PRAISE FOR *REVENGE*

"It's not just Murakami but also the shadow of Borges that hovers over this mesmerizing book . . . One may detect a slight bow to the American macabre of E. A. Poe. Ogawa stands on the shoulders of giants, as another saying goes. But this collection may linger in your mind—it does in mine—as a delicious, perplexing, absorbing and somehow singular experience." —Alan Cheuse, NPR

"A secret garden of dark, glorious flowers: silky, heart-breakingly beautiful . . . and poison to their roots."

—Joe Hill, author of *Heart-Shaped Box* and *NOS4A2*

"Yoko Ogawa is an absolute master of the gothic at its most beautiful and dangerous, and *Revenge* is a collection that deepens and darkens with every story you read."

—Peter Straub, author of *Lost Boy, Lost Girl* and *Ghost Story*

"[Ogawa] stresses the trustworthiness of the storyteller and the essential reality of what we are seeing, even as strange situations and surreal events create a dreamlike undertow, challenging our sense of security. The result is a profound unease that spreads out and permeates the narrative. Kafka is, of course, one of the great disseminators of this technique, and Murakami also uses it, but Ogawa makes it her own, with excellent results."

—Robert Siegel, *Los Angeles Review of Books*

"Magnificently macabre . . . [Ogawa] is the Japanese master of dread . . . These tales are not for the faint of heart, but Ms. Ogawa is more 'Masque of the Red Death' than she is *The Ring*. She elevates herself above any limitations of the genre she's working in."

—Zoë Lescaze, *Observer* (New York)

"Equally seductive and unsettling, these tales overwhelm the reader with sinister dreamscapes, each exquisitely rendered in cool, precise prose that has been rightfully compared to that of fellow Japanese author Haruki Murakami . . . Her tales will long linger in the mind."

—John McMurtrie, *SFGate*

"If creepy were a place, Ms. Ogawa has come up with many ways to get there . . . Even while punctuated [by] macabre flourishes [her] book maintains its restraint, like a dark alley that's too quiet."

—Susannah Meadows, *The New York Times*

"Every act of malice glows creepily against the plain background. [*Revenge* is] a book that ought to be distributed to every fiction-M.F.A. candidate who tends to overwrite: Ogawa is an expert in doing more with less."

—*New York*

"Reading Yoko Ogawa is akin to watching a film by David Lynch; the experience is an admixture of vertiginous revelation and dark defamiliarization . . . Her stories seem to exist in a timeless, fluid medium all its own."

—Rhoda Feng, *HuffPost*

“Ogawa’s language, in Stephen Snyder’s translation, is spare, quiet, content with being nimble rather than dwelling on beautiful phrases. It’s a language that doesn’t announce its own frugality and refuses to make a minimalist’s daring and obvious cuts. The seeming ease is the outcome of hard work, but it doesn’t make the reader sweat. Ogawa moves swiftly; she has the power to move.”

—Stefan Kiesbye, *Los Angeles Review of Books*

“Woven through the eleven interconnected tales is a thread of the grotesque, the macabre, the mournful . . . [Ogawa’s] language is both spare and searingly precise, crystallizing the details of everyday existence and capturing the unexpected shock of the bizarre . . . Readers willing to explore the murkier edges of the human psyche will not be disappointed.” —Monica Rhor, Associated Press

“Disturbing . . . The delicate, slow-burning eeriness [lingers] long after the book is put down.”

—*Time Out New York*

YOKO OGAWA

REVENGE

Translated by Stephen Snyder

Yoko Ogawa is the author of *Mina's Matchbox*, *The Memory Police*, *Hotel Iris*, *The Housekeeper and the Professor*, and *The Diving Pool.* Her fiction has appeared in *The New Yorker*, *A Public Space*, and *Zoetrope.* Since 1988 she has published more than twenty works of fiction and nonfiction and has won every major Japanese literary award. Her novel *The Housekeeper and the Professor* was adapted into the 2006 film *The Professor's Beloved Equation.* She lives in Ashiya, Japan, with her husband and son.

Stephen Snyder teaches Japanese literature at Middlebury College. His translations include works by Kenzaburō Ōe, Ryu Murakami, Natsuo Kirino, and Miri Yu.

Also by Yoko Ogawa

Mina's Matchbox

The Memory Police

Hotel Iris

The Housekeeper and the Professor

The Diving Pool

REVENGE

REVENGE

ELEVEN DARK TALES

YOKO OGAWA

TRANSLATED FROM THE JAPANESE BY

STEPHEN SNYDER

With a New Introduction by

CARMEN MARIA MACHADO

PICADOR • NEW YORK

Picador
120 Broadway, New York 10271

EU Representative: Macmillan Publishers Ireland Ltd, 1st Floor, The Liffey Trust Centre, 117–126 Sheriff Street Upper, Dublin 1, DO1 YC43

Originally published in Japanese in 1998 by Jitsugyo no Nihon Sha, Japan, as *Kamoku na shigai, midara na tomurai*
English translation originally published in the United States in 2013 by Picador
Paperback reissue edition, 2025

"Old Mrs. J" originally appeared in *Harper's Magazine*, in slightly different form. "Afternoon at the Bakery" appeared in *Zoetrope: All-Story*. "The Last Hour of the Bengal Tiger" appeared in *Guernica*.

Library of Congress Control Number: 2012037099
2025 paperback ISBN: 978-1-250-37598-8

Designed by Steven Seighman

10 9 8 7 6 5 4 3 2 1

CONTENTS

INTRODUCTION

by Carmen María Machado

I first read Yoko Ogawa's *Revenge* a year or two out of graduate school. The copy that lives on my shelf is thick with embarrassing annotations—practically juvenilia. I had to get a new copy to write this introduction; I couldn't even bear to look at them.

Back then, I was still learning how to articulate fiction's power. I did not quite know what to make of these spare, surreal, elliptical stories, which felt disarmingly vital and alive in ways I didn't understand. For years, I recommended and taught *Revenge* more times than I could count, even while its mysteries eluded me. Where, I wondered, as I tore through the collection for the second, third, fourth time, was this book's engine? What made it tick? What called to me from its pages?

You could say I wanted to take it apart. You could say I wanted to see what was inside.

In the opening story of *Revenge*, a woman walks into a pristine but unmanned bakery and waits to be served. She meditates on the plaza outside, the bustle of families and pigeons and stray cats and passersby. The scene is gentle, almost serene. Then comes the final sentence of the first section: "You could gaze at this perfect picture all day—an afternoon bathed in light and comfort—and perhaps never notice a single detail out of place, or missing."

Soothing imagery punctuated by a note of disquiet is Ogawa's specialty, as are spasms of perverse humor. Female characters sit in seemingly endless wells of poise and reserve, only to lash out with shocking violence. Grief and alienation calcify into horror. An aura of dread hovers around every scene. Every new paragraph could bring a nightmarish detail or the saddest story you've ever heard. Or maybe both. Each story autopsies the space between characters who do not understand each other: A customer and an employee. A boy and his young stepmother. Classmates, coworkers, neighbors, strangers, lovers. No one is safe from Ogawa's roving scalpel. The horrors never feel far away; they are domestic, intimate, unbearably close.

The protagonists in *Revenge* never repeat but move between stories, appearing in unexpected places and revealing surprising connective tissue. A bakery employee in the first story appears as a younger woman in the second. A snowstorm that delays a train in one story—keeping a young man from his stepmother's funeral—also delays a doctor, leading to his grisly end. The doctor's downstairs neighbor, who is unnerved by but obsessed with his death, is hypnotized by the discovery of a dead hamster in a public trash can. The person who left the hamster in the trash can has their own agenda with someone else in the dead doctor's hospital. A dying tiger in one story is a disintegrating fur coat in another. A writer and her doomed projects, appearing multiple times, generate moments of genuine metafictional slipperiness—including one where she begins to read from her own book, which contains passages of the book in which she resides, which is to say, the one we are reading, which is to say, the one you are about to read. And all the stories are linked by dreamlike, eerie, or morbid images of food, animals, and domesticity—a road thick with flawless tomatoes,[*] an abandoned post office full of kiwis, carrots in the unmistakable shape of human hands,[†] moldy strawberry cakes,[‡] rotten and liquified scallops, a fridge with a terrible secret inside.

The different threads coil and tangle, vanish, and reappear unexpectedly, often around your throat. Then the end loops back to the beginning; it can start all over again. It can—if you let it—go on forever.

Yoko Ogawa's career—which has spanned over four decades and over fifty books of fiction and nonfiction—

[*] A driver, moving through them, wonders, "Did hitting tomatoes feel the same as hitting a person? I began to count: one, two, three, four, five . . ." The tomatoes also appear elsewhere, in a salad.

[†] "Scrubbing turned it bright red."

[‡] "It was like breathing in death."

began when she was studying literature at Waseda University in Tokyo. After marrying her husband, an engineer, she continued to write. In 2024, she told a journalist that her husband didn't even know she was a writer until her debut novel, *The Breaking of the Butterfly*, won a literary prize. "He was at work, I was at home, it didn't seem relevant," she said. "He was quite surprised when he found out that I'd written something."

Originally published as 寡黙な死骸みだらな弔い (*Kamoku na shigai, midara na tomurai*) in 1998, *Revenge* continued themes that occupied much of Ogawa's early career, argues Dr. Grace En-Yi Ting in her essay "Ogawa Yōko and the Horrific Femininities of Daily Life." These themes—"improper femininities," "disregard[ed] boundaries," and the "unpleasant realities of domestic spaces"—would not seem, at first glance, to be obvious themes for a work of horror. The American translation released by Picador in 2013 was marketed explicitly to such readers: the title is slashed into a filthy surface and beaded with blood. It's probably why I picked it up in the first place. But now, in 2025, fully familiar with the sensation of demurring when pressed on the question of the genre of my own work, I see how books like *Revenge* really underline the futility of taxonomy. It's a feminist poioumenon, a surreal gothic, a domestic horror, a playful and nightmarish Borromean knot. There is not much here for splattergore enthusiasts; the horror in *Revenge* is gradual, accreted, like dust and skin cells collecting against a baseboard. There are flares of gruesome violence, to be sure, both heightened and controlled by its elegant and poisonous sentences, but much of the dread depends on the interstices, the white space, the way we drift in and out of people's lives and then find them again, much later, utterly changed or unbearably the same.

This is why it can be hard for some writers to answer those questions. After all, who are we to say where our stories live?

The women of *Revenge* are grief obliterated, depressed, murderous, or insane. They talk too much, they dramatize, they overreact. Their sons die or leave them. They lust after the wrong men, which is to say, any man at all. They kill those men, or drive them away, or unsettle them. The men, on the other hand, are linked by everything the women don't have: their rational minds, their dry affects, their passivity, their dismissiveness.

The original title of *Revenge*, translated, is something like *Silent Corpses, Obscene Mourning*. Here, the book's thesis comes into focus: its parade of monstrous, unstable female characters exists to highlight "discourses marking women as overly emotional and illogical," argues Dr. Ting.

"Ogawa creates female characters who truly *have* gone mad, past the point of caring," she writes, "as they are driven off the edge by frustration towards such stereotypes and expectations permeating their everyday lives." Dr. Ting draws a connection between these stories and the glossy, idealized figure of the shufu (主婦), the postwar Japanese housewife, defined by her domestic aspirations, her subjugation, and later, her shallowness and good cheer. Where else can such a character go but to chaos, to abjection, to obscene emotional excess? Where women are "supposed" to nurture and comfort, Dr. Ting says, "distorted forms of intimacy and violence appear." In this way, Ogawa is Murakami (whom she has cited as a major influence in her work) by way of Tillie Olsen: surrealism marshalled to feminist ends.

Stories of the consequences of the trivialization of women's labor and lives have a long history. Rereading *Revenge* in adulthood, I was reminded of the American playwright and novelist Susan Glaspell's 1917 story "A Jury of Her Peers." It, too, shoves its fingers into the suppurating wound of gender politics and women's spaces: a group of rational men serenely take in a murder scene, attempting to locate a motive for a farmer's strangulation, while the women, restricted to the kitchen, solve the crime and conceal the evidence, determining silently between them that the incarcerated wife was justified in her actions. Perhaps not by accident, this story, too, contains dead animals (a throttled bird), disturbing images of food (sticky preserves speckled with shards of glass), and disrupted domestic life ("'Nothing here but kitchen things,'" the sheriff says, "with a little laugh for the insignificance of kitchen things").

We have become more open to the discussion of female rage even as reactionary jaws close around us. It has become ubiquitous, almost memeified. I can't count the number of fancams and clip compilations I've seen joyfully highlighting this extremely specific mood—shots of a grief-drunk Florence Pugh (*Midsommar*), a deranged-with-rejection Mia Goth (*Pearl*), an enraged Toni Collette (*Hereditary*), a contemptuous Sandra Hüller (*Anatomy of a Fall*). There is something wildly satisfying about their bad behavior, their loudly articulated grievances, and their dark, specific desires. After all, what else is to be done? The twin specters of men's violence and men's contempt—eternal, unrelenting—have rendered any response, no matter how extreme, utterly reasonable.

The madwoman in the attic is not someone to be locked away or feared. We need her. We have always needed her.

March 2025
Iowa City, IA

REVENGE

AFTERNOON AT THE BAKERY

It was a beautiful Sunday. The sky was a cloudless dome of sunlight. Out on the square, leaves fluttered in a gentle breeze along the pavement. Everything seemed to glimmer with a faint luminescence: the roof of the ice-cream stand, the faucet on the drinking fountain, the eyes of a stray cat, even the base of the clock tower covered with pigeon droppings.

Families and tourists strolled through the square, enjoying the weekend. Squeaky sounds could be heard from a man off in the corner, who was twisting balloon animals. A circle of children watched him, entranced. Nearby, a woman sat on a bench knitting. Somewhere a horn sounded. A flock of pigeons burst into the air, and startled a baby who began to cry. The mother hurried over to gather the child in her arms.

You could gaze at this perfect picture all day—an

afternoon bathed in light and comfort—and perhaps never notice a single detail out of place, or missing.

As I pushed through the revolving door of the bakery and walked inside, the noise of the square was instantly muffled, and replaced by the sweet scent of vanilla. The shop was empty.

"Excuse me," I called hesitantly. There was no reply, so I decided to sit down on a stool in the corner and wait.

It was my first time in the bakery, a neat, clean, modest little shop. Cakes, pies, and chocolates were carefully arranged in a glass case, and tins of cookies lined shelves on either side. On the counter behind the register was a roll of pretty orange and light blue checkered wrapping paper.

Everything looked delicious. But I knew before I entered the shop what I would buy: two strawberry shortcakes. That was all.

The bell in the clock tower rang four times. Once more a flock of pigeons rose into the sky and flew across the square, settling in front of the flower shop. The florist came out with a scowl on her face and a mop to drive them away, and a flurry of gray feathers wafted into the air.

There was no sign of anyone in the shop, and after waiting a little while longer I considered giving up and leaving. But I had only recently moved to this town and I did not know of another good bakery. Perhaps the fact that they could keep customers waiting like this was a sign of confidence, rather than rudeness. The light in the glass display case was pleasant and soft, the pastries looked beautiful, and the stool was quite comfortable—I liked the place, in spite of the service.

A short, plump woman stepped from the revolving door. Noise from the square filtered in behind her and faded away. "Is anybody here?" she called out. "Where could she have gone?" she added, turning and smiling at me. "She must be out on an errand. I'm sure she'll be right back." She sat down next to me and I gave a little bow.

"I suppose I could get behind the counter and serve you myself," the woman said. "I know pretty well how things work around here, I sell them their spices."

"That's very kind of you, but I'm not in a hurry," I said.

We waited together. She rearranged her scarf, tapped the toe of her shoe, and anxiously fidgeted with the clasp on a black leather wallet—apparently used to collect her accounts. I realized she was trying to come up with a topic for conversation.

"The cakes here are delicious," she said at last. "They use our spices, so you know there's nothing funny in them."

"That's reassuring," I said.

"The place is usually very busy. Strange that it's so empty today. There's often a line outside."

People passed by the shop window—young couples, old men, tourists, a policeman on patrol—but no one seemed interested in the bakery. The woman turned to look out at the square, and ran her fingers through her wavy white hair. Whenever she moved in her seat, she gave off an odd smell; the scent of medicinal herbs and overripe fruit mingled with the vinyl of her apron. It reminded me of when I was a child, and the smell of the little greenhouse in the garden where my father used to raise orchids. I was strictly forbidden to open the door; but once, without permission, I did. The scent of the orchids was not at all disagreeable, and this pleasant association made me like the old woman.

"I was happy to see they have strawberry shortcake," I said, pointing at the case. "They're the real thing. None of that jelly, or too much fruit piled on top, or those little figurines they use for decoration. Just strawberries and cream."

"You're right," she said. "I can guarantee they're good. The best thing in the shop. The base is made with our special vanilla."

"I'm buying them for my son. Today is his birthday."

"Really? Well, I hope it's a happy one. How old is he?"

"Six. He'll always be six. He's dead."

He died twelve years ago. Suffocated in an abandoned refrigerator left in a vacant lot. When I first saw him, I didn't think he was dead. I thought he was just ashamed to look me in the eye because he had stayed away from home for three days.

An old woman I had never seen before was standing nearby, looking dazed, and I realized that she must have been the one who had found him. Her hair was disheveled, her face pale, and her lips were trembling. She looked more dead than my son.

"I'm not angry, you know," I said to him. "Come here and let me give you a hug. I bought the shortcake for your birthday. Let's go back to the house."

But he didn't move. He had curled up in an ingenious

fashion to fit between the shelves and the egg box, with his legs carefully folded and his face tucked between his knees. The curve of his spine receded into a dark, cramped space behind him that I could not see. The skin on his neck caught the light from the open door. It was so smooth, covered in soft down—I knew it all too well.

"No, it couldn't be," I said to the old woman nearby. "He's just sleeping. He hasn't eaten anything, and he must be exhausted. Let's carry him home and try not to wake him. He should sleep, as much as he wants. He'll wake up later, I'm sure of it."

But the woman did not answer.

The reaction of the woman in the shop to my story was unlike anything I'd encountered in the past. There was no sign of sympathy or surprise or even embarrassment on her face. I would have known if she was merely pretending to respond so placidly. The experience of losing my son had taught me to read people, and I could tell immediately that this woman was genuine. She neither regretted having asked me the question nor blamed me for confessing something so personal to a stranger.

"Well," she said, "then it was lucky you chose this bakery. There are no better pastries anywhere; your son will be pleased. And they include a whole box of birthday candles for free. They're darling—red, blue, pink, yellow, some with flowers or butterflies, animals, anything you could want."

She smiled faintly, in a way that seemed perfectly suited to the quiet of the bakery. I found myself wondering whether she understood that my son had died. Or perhaps she knew only too well about people dying.

Long after I had realized that my son would not be coming back, I kept the strawberry shortcake we were meant to have eaten together. I passed my days watching it rot. First, the cream turned brown and separated from the fat, staining the cellophane wrapper. Then the strawberries dried out, wrinkling up like the heads of deformed babies. The sponge cake hardened and crumbled, and finally a layer of mold appeared.

"Mold can be quite beautiful," I told my husband. The spots multiplied, covering the shortcake in delicate blotches of color.

"Get rid of it," my husband said.

I could tell he was angry. But I did not understand why he would speak so harshly about our son's birthday cake. So I threw it in his face. Mold and crumbs covered his hair and his cheeks, and a terrible smell filled the room. It was like breathing in death.

The strawberry shortcakes were displayed right on the upper shelf of the pastry case, the most prominent place in the shop. Each was topped with three whole strawberries. They looked perfectly preserved, no sign of mold.

"I think I'll be going," the old woman said. She stood up, smoothed her apron, and glanced out the window toward the square, as though looking one last time for the return of the bakery shop girl.

"I'll wait a little longer," I said.

"You do that," she said, reaching out to gently touch my hand. Hers was callused and wrinkled—made rough by her work—and she had dirt under her fingernails. Still, her hand was warm and comforting, perhaps like the heat from those little birthday candles she had mentioned. "I'm going to check on a couple of places where the girl might be, and if I find her I'll tell her to come straight back."

"Thank you," I said.

"Not at all . . . Good-bye."

Clutching her wallet under her arm, she turned to leave. As she stepped through the revolving door, I noticed that her apron strings were coming untied in the back. I tried to stop her, but I was too late. She disappeared into the crowd in the square, and I was alone again.

He was an intelligent child. He could read his favorite picture book from beginning to end aloud without making a single mistake. He would use a different voice for each character—the piglet, the prince, the robot, the old man. He was left-handed. He had a broad forehead and a mole on one earlobe. When I was busy making dinner, he would often ask questions I did not know how to answer. Who invented Chinese characters? Why do people grow? What is air? Where do we go when we die?

After he was gone, I began to collect newspaper

clippings about children who had died under tragic circumstances. Each day I would go to the library and gather articles from every newspaper and magazine, and then make copies of them.

An eleven-year-old girl who was raped and buried in a forest. A nine-year-old boy abducted by a deviant and later found in a wine crate with both of his ankles severed. A ten-year-old on a tour of an ironworks who slipped from a catwalk and was instantly dissolved in the smelter. I would read these articles aloud, reciting them like poems.

How had I not noticed before? I rose slightly from my seat and looked past the counter. A doorway behind the cash register was half open, and I could see into the kitchen. A young woman was standing inside with her face turned away. I was about to call out to her, but I stopped myself. She was talking to someone on the telephone, and she was crying.

I couldn't hear anything, but I could see her shoulders trembling. Her hair had been gathered carelessly under a white cap. Despite some spots of cream and chocolate, her apron looked neat and pressed. Her slight frame seemed almost that of a little girl.

I returned to my stool and looked out at the square. The balloon seller was still making animals for the children. Pigeons were clustered here and there, and the woman was still knitting on the bench. Nothing appeared to have changed, except that the shadow of the clock tower had grown longer and thinner.

The kitchen was as neatly arranged as the shop. Bowls, knives, mixers, pastry bags, sifters—everything needed for the work of the day was right where it should be. The dish-towels were clean and dry, the floor spotless. And in the middle of it stood the girl, her sadness perfectly at home in the tidy kitchen. I could hear nothing, not a word, not a sound. Her hair swayed slightly with her sobs. She was looking down at the counter, her body leaning against the oven. Her right hand clutched a napkin. I couldn't see the expression on her face, but her misery was clear from the clench of her jaw, the pallor of her neck, and the tense grip of her fingers on the telephone.

The reason she was crying didn't matter to me. Perhaps there was no reason at all. Her tears had that sort of purity.

The door that would not open no matter how hard you pushed, no matter how long you pounded on it. The screams no one heard. Darkness, hunger, pain. Slow suffocation. One day it occurred to me that I needed to experience the same suffering he had.

First, I turned off our refrigerator and emptied it: last night's potato salad, ham, eggs, cabbage, cucumbers, wilted spinach, yogurt, some cans of beer, pork—I pulled everything out and threw it aside. The ketchup spilled, eggs broke, ice cream melted. But the refrigerator was empty now, so I took a deep breath, curled myself into a ball, and slowly worked my way inside.

As the door closed, all light vanished. I could no longer tell whether my eyes were open or shut, and I realized that it made no difference in here. The walls of the refrigerator were still cool. Where does death come from?

"What do you think you're doing?" my husband said as he ripped open the refrigerator door.

"I'm going to him." I tried to brush away his shaking hand and close the door again.

"That's enough," he said, pulling me from the refrigerator. He slapped my face. Then he left me.

Not one person in the crowd on the square knew that a young woman was crying in the kitchen behind the bakery. I was the only witness.

The afternoon sunlight streaming in through the window had darkened, as the sun began to dip below the roof of the town hall. The man on the square with the popular balloon animals performed now for only a few children. A group of people had gathered around the clock tower to take pictures of the automaton show as the bell struck five.

I knew I had only to call out to the girl, and then I could make my purchase and leave, but I refrained. Her starched apron was slightly too large, which made her seem all the more small and vulnerable. I noticed the perspiration on her neck, her wrinkled cuffs and long fingers, and I imagined how she must look when she is working. I could see her taking the steaming sponge cakes from the oven, piping on the cream, and arranging each strawberry with infinite care. I was certain she would make the finest shortcakes in the world.

Several years after my son died, when I began living alone, I received an odd phone call. The voice was unfamiliar but clearly that of a young man. He sounded a little nervous, yet he spoke politely as he mentioned my son's name.

"What?" I gasped, for a moment paralyzed.

"Is he at home?" he said.

"No, he's not," I managed to say.

"Well then . . . I just wanted to speak to him about the reunion. For our middle school class. Do you know when he'll be back?"

I told him he wasn't home, that he's living abroad, going to school.

"Oh, that's too bad," he said. "I was looking forward to seeing him." He sounded genuinely disappointed.

"Were you friends?"

"Yes. We were in the theater club together. He was president and I was vice president."

"The theater club?"

"We won the city competition and went on to the nationals. You remember, we did *Man of Flame*. He played Van Gogh, and I played his brother, Theo. He was always the leading man, the ladies' man, and I was his sidekick. Not just on stage but in life. He was always in the limelight."

Somehow it didn't bother me that he was talking about

a completely different person. Nor did I try to correct him. My son had read his picture books so well that it seemed quite likely he might have had a leading role in a play one day.

"Is he still acting?"

"Yes—"

"Really? I thought so. Could you tell him I called?"

"Of course, I will."

After he had hung up, I held the phone to my ear for a moment, listening to the hum of the dial tone. I never heard from him again.

The bell in the clock tower began to ring. A flock of pigeons lifted into the sky. As the fifth chime sounded, a door beneath the clock opened and a little parade of animated figurines pirouetted out—a few soldiers, a chicken, and a skeleton. Since the clock was very old, the figurines were slightly discolored, their movements stiff and awkward. The chicken's head swiveled about as if to squawk; the skeleton danced. And then, from the door, an angel appeared, beating her golden wings.

The girl in the kitchen replaced the receiver. I held my breath. She looked down at the phone for a moment, then she heaved a deep sigh and dabbed at her tears with the napkin.

I repeated to myself what I would say when she emerged into the fading light of the shop: "Two strawberry shortcakes, please."

FRUIT JUICE

It was late in the day, and classes had ended. The library was nearly empty. I sat in a quiet corner, studying, when she appeared from nowhere and startled me out of my book.

"Are you busy this Sunday?" she asked.

Her question flustered me for a moment, I didn't know what to say. She was staring down at the floor, half hidden behind a bookshelf.

"If you have plans, of course, don't worry about it." She held a book in her hand, and absentmindedly rubbed her palm along its spine. I knew her from class, but we had never spoken before, and I had never been this close to her.

"No, I'm not busy," I said rather brusquely, to hide my confusion.

"Well . . . I was hoping you'd come with me somewhere."

Was she asking me out? That seemed to be where this

was going. If so, I had no objections. She seemed nice enough. At the same time, though, I knew better than to jump to conclusions—and her invitation felt more like an apology than an attempt at flirtation.

"Where are we going?" I asked.

"To a French restaurant," she said with some hesitation, her eyes still fixed on the floor. "I don't want to go, but I have to. We'll have lunch . . . that's about it. It'll be painless." Her whole body seemed to shrink with each word she spoke, as though she hoped to hide behind that bookshelf, deep in the shadows of the library. "I know this must seem kind of random. Just tell me if you don't want to go."

Sunlight streamed in through the window to the west, turning her long hair amber. I could hear in the distance the sound of basketballs bouncing against the gymnasium floor.

"Sure, I'd be happy to go," I said. "Just to have lunch, right? Why not?"

I resisted the urge to press for details, or to ask why she had chosen me of all people to go with her. I worried that if she were forced to say more, she might shrink farther away and disappear altogether.

"Thank you," she said, with obvious relief. Then, at last, she looked up and smiled slightly, but I felt a pang of disappointment.

"My mother is sick," the girl told me in the subway on the way to the restaurant. "Did you know she's in the hospital?" I shook my head. I had heard that she lived alone with her mother, but that was all I knew about her. A rumor had circulated around school that she was someone's illegitimate child. I didn't remember much about it.

"She has liver cancer. She won't live much longer." Her words were clear and audible over the rumbling of the subway. "The other day she told me that if anything happened to her I should contact this man, that he would help me."

She pulled a business card from her skirt pocket. It was printed with the name of a relatively well-known politician, a man who had recently served in some important post, as minister of labor or perhaps postmaster general. The edges of the card were creased and worn, as though her mother had been keeping it for some time.

"How bad is she?" I asked, not knowing quite what to say. I was afraid of hurting her.

"Four months in the hospital. I've been home alone all that time."

She was wearing a blouse with a floral pattern and a skirt of some soft material. The collar and cuffs of the blouse were neatly ironed. She looked older in these clothes than she did in her school uniform.

She was an inconspicuous girl, perhaps the quietest in our grade. She almost never spoke in class, and when asked to stand up and translate a passage from English, or to solve a math problem on the board, she did it as discreetly as possible, without fuss. She had no friends to speak of, belonged to no clubs, and she ate her lunch in a corner by herself.

Still, no one bullied her or treated her like an outcast. She wasn't disagreeable, just easy to ignore. You could even say her silence suited her. The pale skin, the long, straight hair, the shadows under her eyes when she bowed her head—it all lent her a kind of tranquillity that I think we didn't want to disturb.

But when someone did take notice of her, it seemed she was always apologizing for it—I suppose "apologetic" might be the best word to describe her. "I'm sorry, please ignore me . . ." You could almost hear her murmur the words, like an incantation, a way of conjuring a still place for herself.

"Are you meeting him for the first time today?" I asked, glancing down at the business card in her hand.

"Yes."

"He never came to see you, even when you were little?"

"Never," she said, shaking her head.

She was so close to me I wondered if she could feel my breath. The card trembled in her hand.

A waiter led us into a private room at the back of the restaurant, where the man was already seated at a table too large for three, sipping a garish red cocktail. For some reason I had assumed he would be accompanied by a secretary or a bodyguard, but he was alone.

A chandelier hung from the ceiling and flowers had been arranged around the room. The silverware gleamed, the tablecloth was blindingly white.

They barely greeted each other, exchanging little more than vague, meaningless grunts. She sat down without introducing me, and I realized the moment for such formalities had already passed.

Sitting with her back straight, she studied the menu

from top to bottom, though she seemed to have little interest in selecting something to eat. This went on for a while. "Order whatever you like," the man repeated several times, just to break the unbearable tension, but she was intent to make him stew in silence. I ran my finger along the edge of the elaborately folded napkin.

"Is there anything you don't like to eat?" he asked.

"No," we said at nearly the same time.

He ordered a great deal of food, speaking so quickly that the waiter could barely keep up. Clearly he was accustomed to giving orders. The dishes arrived one after another and we made short work of them, our chewing and swallowing the only sound in the room. The man downed another drink.

He was short and solidly built, but he looked older than he did on television. His hair was thinning and the skin on his neck sagged. There were liver spots on his face and hands.

I would have expected a man of his power and position to be more arrogant or condescending, but his daughter had fully succeeded in making him uncomfortable. He groped for topics of conversation and was disconcerted when nothing succeeded in coaxing a response.

"What's your favorite subject in school?" he said. It was the kind of question you asked a child, and it occurred to me that there were more important topics he might have broached—her mother's condition, their economic difficulties, perhaps the apology he owed them. I began to worry that my presence was inhibiting him, making things complicated.

"Classics," she said, setting down her knife and fork and wiping her mouth with her napkin. "And English . . . and music. I guess music is my favorite."

"Music, is it? That's fine. How about you?" he asked me.

I blurted out "Biology" for lack of anything better to say. Biology, P.E.—What did it matter? We were just talking to fill the silence.

"Do you play a sport?"

"No, not really."

"Ah, they've used truffles in this consommé," he suddenly remarked with obvious pleasure. "Do you like them?"

"I've never had them before."

"They're something of an acquired taste. . . . And what do you do when you're not in school?"

"Play with the cat, do the laundry, listen to music—stuff like that."

The waiter brought out the fish course. The man had ordered sea bream with a pea-green sauce; his daughter had scallops meunière, I had a steamed lobster.

She ate with impeccable table manners, her back straight, her knees flush together, her feet planted evenly on the floor. She kept her eyes on her plate, and raised them only when answering a question and then only slightly, as though she were looking at a spot near the butter dish at the center of the table.

I glanced over at her whenever I had the chance. Her hair fell in dainty wisps around her face. She had nice features—an intelligent brow, a firm jaw—but she was difficult to read. On the one hand, she could be pretty tough on her father, but at the same time she was her usual apologetic self. She seemed to doubt that she was worthy to be eating these delicious scallops, or even to be here at the table.

Next came the meat course, served with a flourish by several waiters. I was already full, but the two of them went on eating almost greedily, so I forced myself to eat the meat as well.

"Do you play an instrument?" he asked. "The piano? The guitar? The violin, perhaps?"

"No," she said. "We don't have any instruments at home."

He coughed, then his knife struck the plate with a harsh clatter. She shook her head, dismissing him.

I suddenly recalled that I'd spoken with this girl once before, at the beginning of third grade. Why had I forgotten it until now? It was after classes had ended for the day. I was passing the music room, but I stopped, sensing someone was inside. When I looked in, she was standing on tiptoe, reaching up to open the glass door of a cabinet. She was alone. I don't know why I stood there watching her. I must have been curious. Or perhaps it was the glimpse of snow-white skin I saw on her wrist as she raised her arm. The cabinet door creaked and she took a deep breath as she reached for the violin inside. She examined it, almost fearfully, and then clutched it to her chest. "What are you doing?" I said. But I shouldn't have interrupted her; I should have left her alone with the violin. She jumped at the sound of my voice. "Nothing," she said, "I'm not doing anything," and hurriedly replaced the violin in the cabinet. One of the strings must have struck the door, and a sound like the cry of a small bird floated across the room.

Dessert arrived: strawberry cake covered in a thick layer of whipped cream. The man wadded up his stained napkin and set it on the table.

"You're welcome to your father's as well," he said, sliding his plate toward her.

An icy gust seemed to pass between them, and the word "father" hung in the air. I glanced over again and saw her devouring her cake, lips shiny with cream.

"No, thank you," she said.

The man insisted on driving us home in the expensive black sedan he had parked in front of the restaurant, but she politely refused. We started walking, but when we came to the subway stop near the restaurant, she marched right past it and we continued on by foot all the way back to our neighborhood. She walked quickly, clutching the strap of her shoulder bag, eyes down on the sidewalk, and she said not a word the entire way.

I was afraid she was angry with me. She had brought me along, but I had been of no use whatsoever. I had eaten my fill of the fancy lunch but done nothing to make the meeting with her father any easier.

I tried to keep up with her, but not get too close, and I searched my head for something to say that might comfort her. But nothing came to me.

The sun began to set, and the sky turned a deep red. Some children flew past us on their bikes, heading home from the park. The sound of laughter on a television came from a house nearby. I caught a glimpse of a stray cat, its tail flicking as it darted down an alley. Though the evening was still, her hair fluttered beautifully, and I could see her ears, pale and transparent like the skin I had glimpsed that day in the music room. They bore no resemblance to those of the man at the restaurant. My chest felt tight. It seemed so many things—the unfamiliar food, the silence—were making me restless.

At last, and without warning, she stopped, like a windup toy that has run down.

"Thank you," she said, looking back at me. Her voice was hoarse, she sounded exhausted.

We sat down for a moment on the steps of an old building. There was a barbershop across the way, and a nursery school beyond that. Behind the buildings there sloped a small hill that had been planted with fruit trees. A motorcycle passed, then someone walking a dog, but there was little here to disturb us.

"We should rest a bit," I said.

"You're right," she said, smoothing her skirt. The soft material brushed against my leg. Her face was disappearing in the dusk. The sweat on my back gave me a chill.

"Where is your mother?" I asked.

"Chuo Hospital."

"I'd like to visit her," I said.

"Really? That would be wonderful. I'm sure she'd be pleased. She gets so lonely."

An ant crawled between our shoes on the hard concrete steps.

"My mother is a typist," she said, looking up at me. "A really good one. The fastest and most accurate in her office. She can type anything—letters, reports, the minutes of a meeting. She's even won prizes for it. Her fingers are perfect, long and very flexible."

"You have beautiful fingers, too," I said, looking down at her hands where they rested on her lap.

"She didn't start out wanting to be a typist. She wanted to play an instrument—and I'm sure she would have been really good at music."

The stray note from the violin in the music room seemed to echo in my ears.

"This used to be a post office," she said, as if to quiet the sound in my head. She nodded at the building behind us. "A long time ago, when we were in kindergarten."

A rusted sign hung above the door, the characters for "post office" barely legible.

The door was locked up with a chain, but just slightly ajar. She peered inside through the narrow opening. "Look!" she called, sounding happier than she had all afternoon.

I put my eye to the crack as well, and at first I could see nothing in the dim light. Gradually, as my eyes adjusted, the inside of the building came into focus.

"Weird . . . ," I murmured. The building was filled almost to the ceiling with piles of small, dark spheres of some sort, like tennis balls.

"Kiwis," she said.

"Kiwis?" I repeated.

Strand Book Store
828 Broadway
New York, New York 10003
212.473.1452

strandbooks.com
strand@strandbooks.com

Sale: 12606783
Date: 04-24-2026
Time: 02:11 PM

Revenge: Eleven Dark Tales
1250375983 Item: $18.00 $18.00

1 Items	Subtotal:	$18.00
	Sales Tax (8.88%):	$1.60
	Total:	$19.60

Credit Card Integrated (AmericanExpress):	$19.00
VALUED CUSTOMER	
AID:	A000000025
Application Label:	AMEX CRED
Card Expiry Date:	03/29
Amount Tendered:	$19.60
Change Due:	$0.00

Printed by: cassandrag
Register: Reg6-Shift1

April 24, 2026 02:11 PM

All books and merchandise in original condition
are eligible for a refund if
returned within 5 days of purchase.

Receipts must accompany all returns
and exchanges.

All clearance items are final sale.

Follow us on all platforms @strandbookstore
Visit our other locations:
450 Columbus Ave
2020 Broadway
60th St & 5th Ave
Happy Reading!

"Let's have a look."

"But it's locked."

"Who cares?" she said, and then she picked up a rock and began to pound at the chain. Her composure vanished as she viciously struck it over and over, until at last it snapped and the door swung open. We stepped inside.

Indeed, they were kiwis, just like the ones they sell at the grocery store. But the scene before us was grotesque and dizzying. We moved slowly into the room, which was cluttered with shelves and desks and cardboard boxes. A pencil sharpener, a red ink pad, and a dusty scale sat on the counter. But the rest of the space was filled with kiwis, enormous heaps of them. The air was both sweet and sour. She reached down to pick up a piece of fruit. I watched, afraid she might disturb the pile and bring it tumbling down on us.

The kiwi was perfect, not a bruise or a blemish anywhere.

"Don't they look delicious?" she said, gazing at the mountain of fruit. "More than you could ever eat!" Then she bit into the one in her hand. I could hear her teeth sink into the flesh.

For a long time, she stood there eating kiwis, one after another. She consumed them like a starving child, dizzy with hunger. Her carefully ironed blouse and her beautiful hands grew sticky. I could only watch and wait until she ate through her sadness.

When she showed up for school on Monday, she was once more the unremarkable girl I had always known. We never spoke after that day.

Her mother died at the start of winter vacation, and I had not kept my promise to visit her in the hospital.

Rather than continuing on to university, the girl went to a cooking school that specialized in pastry-making. The last time I saw her was at graduation. Some twenty years have passed since our lunch with her father. That Sunday—and the moment in the music room—sank into a hole at the bottom of my sea of memories.

I did phone her once, however, five or six years later, when I came across an obituary for the man we had dined with at the French restaurant. The phone number of the bakery where she was working was in the alumni register.

"I'm afraid I wasn't much use to you that day," I said.

"No, you can't imagine how it helped to have you there. I mean it. I'm truly grateful. At the time I . . . I . . ."

She started to cry on the other end of the line. Not because the man was dead. I realized she was finally letting flow the tears she could not cry at the post office, and that this sadness was coming to her peacefully from the distant past.

"I never thanked you properly back then," she said. "I'm sorry."

OLD MRS. J

My new apartment was in a building at the top of a hill. From my window, there was a wonderful view of the town spread out like a fan below and the sea beyond. An editor I knew had recommended the place.

The hill was planted with fruit: a few grapevines and some peach and loquat trees. The rest was all kiwis. The orchards belonged to my landlady, Mrs. J, but she was elderly and lived alone, and she apparently left the trees and vines to themselves. There was no sign of laborers working the orchard, and the hill was always quiet. Nevertheless, the trees were covered with beautiful fruit.

The kiwis in particular grew so thick that on moonlit nights when the wind was blowing, the whole hillside would tremble as though covered with a swarm of dark green bats. At times I found myself thinking they might fly away at any moment.

Then one day I realized that all the kiwis had disappeared from one section of the orchard, though I had seen no one picking them. After a few days the branches were again covered with tiny new fruit. Since I was in the habit of writing at night and sleeping until almost noon, it was possible I had simply missed the workers.

The building was three stories tall and U-shaped. In the center was a spacious garden, with a large eucalyptus tree for shade when the sun was too bright. Mrs. J grew tomatoes, carrots, eggplants, green beans, and peppers, which she shared with her favorite tenants, I assumed.

Her apartment was directly across the courtyard from mine. A single curtain hung in her window; the other was missing and she seemed to be in no hurry to replace it. Whenever I looked up from my desk, I would see that orphaned curtain.

From what I could tell, Mrs. J led a quiet, monotonous life. As I was getting up each day, I could see her through the window sitting down in front of her TV, wearily eating her lunch. If she happened to spill something, she would wipe it up with the tablecloth or her sleeve. After lunch, she would pass the time knitting or polishing pots or simply napping on the couch. And by the evening, when I was at last beginning to get down to work, I would see her changing into a worn-out nightgown and crawling into bed.

I wondered how old she was. Well past eighty, I imagined. She was unsteady on her feet and was constantly bumping into chairs or knocking over something on the table. In the garden, however, she was a different woman;

she seemed years younger and much more at ease when she was watering or staking the plants, or plucking insects with her tweezers. The clicking of her shears as she harvested her crop echoed pleasantly through the courtyard.

A stray cat turned out to be the reason for my first gift of vegetables from Mrs. J.

"Nasty thing!" she screamed, brandishing a shovel. I spotted a cat slinking off toward the orchard. It looked nearly as old as Mrs. J and seemed to be suffering from a skin disease.

I opened the window and called out that she should spread pine needles around the beds, but in response she just turned and walked toward me, apparently still quite angry.

"I can't stand them!" she said. "They dig up the seeds I've just planted, leave their smelly mess in the garden, and then have the nerve to make that terrible racket."

"Pine needles around the beds would keep them away," I repeated.

"Why do you suppose they insist on coming here and ignore all the other yards? I'm allergic to the hair. It gives me sneezing fits."

"Cats hate prickly things," I persisted. "So pine needles—"

"Someone must be feeding them on the sly. If you see anyone leaving food out, would you mind telling them to stop?" As she made this last request, she came marching into my apartment through the kitchen door. Having finished her diatribe against cats, she looked around with poorly disguised curiosity, studying my desk and the cupboard and the glass figurines on the windowsill. "So, you're a 'writer,'" she said, as though she found the word difficult to pronounce.

"That's right."

"Nothing wrong with writing," she said. "It's nice and quiet. A sculptor used to live in this apartment. That was awful. I nearly went deaf from all the pounding." She tapped on her ear and then went over to the bookcase and began reading out titles as she traced the spines with her finger. Yet she got them all wrong—perhaps she was losing her eyesight, or simply did not know how to read.

Mrs. J was extremely slender. Her face was narrow and her chin long and pointed. She had a flat nose, and her eyes were set widely apart in a way that gave the middle of her face a strange blankness. When she spoke, her bones seemed to grind together with each word, and I feared that her dentures might drop out of her head.

"What did your husband do?" I asked.

"My husband? He was nothing but a lousy drunk. I've had to manage for myself, living off the rents from the building, and the money I earn giving massages." Bored with the bookcase, she next went to my word processor and tapped gingerly at a key or two, as though it were a dangerous object. "He gambled away everything I made and didn't even have the decency to die properly. He was drunk and went missing down at the beach."

"I'd love to get a massage when you have time," I said, eager to change the subject for fear she would go on forever about her husband. "I sit all day and my neck gets terribly stiff."

"Of course," she said. "Whenever you like. There's some strength left in these old hands." Then she cracked her knuckles so loudly I thought she might have broken her fingers. As she left, she gave me five peppers she had just picked from her garden.

When I got up the next day, the whole courtyard was covered with pine needles. They were scattered from the trunk of the eucalyptus to the storage shed—everywhere except in the vegetable beds themselves.

I overheard from my window one of the tenants ask about the needles, and Mrs. J explained that they were to keep the cats away. "Cats hate pine tar," she said. "My grandmother taught me that years ago when I was a girl." I wondered whether she had ever been a girl; somehow I felt she had been an old woman from the day she was born.

One evening, Mrs. J had a visitor—apparently a rare occasion. A large, middle-aged man appeared at her apartment. The moon, full and orange, lit up her window more brightly than ever. The man lay down on the bed, and she sat on top of him.

At first I thought she was strangling him. She appeared to have much greater strength than I had realized; she had pinned him down with her weight, and gripped the back of his neck with her powerful hands. It seemed as though he were withering away while she grew more powerful, wringing the life from his body.

The massage lasted quite a long time. The darkness between our two windows was filled with the smell of pine needles.

Mrs. J began to come to my apartment quite often. She would have a cup of tea and chatter on about something—the pain in her knee, the high price of gas, the terrible heat—and then go home again. In the interest of preserving good relations with my landlady, I did my best to be polite. And with each visit she brought more vegetables.

She also began receiving letters and packages for me when I was out.

"This came for you," she'd say, arriving at my door almost before I'd had time to put down my purse. Just as I could see everything that went on in her apartment, she missed nothing that happened in mine. "A delivery truck brought it this afternoon," she added.

"Thank you," I said. "It looks like a friend has sent me some scallops. If you like, I'll bring some over for you later."

"How kind of you! They're my favorite."

But I nearly became ill when I opened the package: the scallops were badly spoiled. The ice pack had long since melted, and they were quite warm. When I pried open a shell with a knife, the scallop and viscera poured out in a liquid mass.

I checked the packing slip and found that they had been sent more than two weeks earlier.

"Look at this!" Mrs. J called as she came barging into my apartment one day.

"What is it?" I asked. I was in the kitchen making potato salad for dinner.

"A carrot," she said, holding it up with obvious pride.

"But what a strange shape," I said, pausing over the potatoes. It was indeed odd: a carrot in the shape of a hand.

It was plump, like a baby's hand, and perfectly formed: five fingers, with a thick thumb and a longer finger in the middle. The greens looked like a scrap of lace decorating the wrist.

"I'd like you to have it," Mrs. J said.

"Are you sure?" I said. "Something this rare?"

"Of course," she said, and put her lips close to my ear to whisper: "I've already found three of them. This one is for you. But don't mention it to anyone; some people might be jealous." I could feel her moist breath. "Is that potato salad?" she added. "Then my timing is perfect: a carrot is just the thing!" She laughed with delight.

I sensed the lingering warmth of the sun as I washed the flesh of the carrot. Scrubbing turned it bright red. I had no idea where to insert the knife, but I decided it would be best to begin by cutting off the five fingers. One by one, they rolled across the cutting board. That evening, my potato salad had bits of the pinkie and the index finger.

The next day, a strong wind blew all through the afternoon and deep into the night. Whirlwinds swept down the hillside and through the orchard. I could sense the trembling of the kiwis.

I was in the kitchen, reading over a manuscript I had recently completed. Whenever I finish a piece, I always read it aloud one last time. But that night I was probably reading to muffle the howl of wind blowing through the branches of the fruit trees.

When I looked up at the window over the sink, I caught sight of a figure in the orchard. Someone was running down the steep slope in the dark. I could see only the back, but I could tell that the person was carrying a large box. When the wind died for a moment, I could even hear the sound of footsteps on the grass. At the bottom of the hill, the figure emerged into the circle of light under a streetlamp and I could see that it was Mrs. J.

Her hair was standing on end. A towel she had tucked into her belt fluttered in the wind, threatening to blow away at any moment. The bottom of the carton she carried was bulging from the weight of its contents. The load was clearly too heavy for a woman of Mrs. J's size, but she seemed to manage it without much difficulty. Eyes front, back straight, she balanced the load with amazing skill—almost as if the box had become a part of her.

I went to the window and stared out. A stronger gust of wind blew through the trees and for a moment Mrs. J lost her footing, but she quickly recovered and moved on. The rustling of the kiwis grew louder.

Mrs. J went into the abandoned post office at the foot of the hill. I had passed it from time to time when I was out for a walk, but I had no idea what it was being used for now or that it belonged to my landlady.

When she finally came back to her apartment, the sea

was beginning to brighten in the east. She got undressed with apparent relief, gargled, pulled a comb through her hair, and put on her old nightgown.

She was once again the Mrs. J I knew—the one who bumped into furniture on the way from the bathroom to her bed, who had trouble simply buttoning her dress. I returned to my reading, the manuscript damp now from the sweat on my palms.

Many more hand-shaped carrots appeared in the days that followed. Even after everyone in the building had received one, there were several left over. Some were long and slender, like the hands of a pianist; others were sturdier, like those of a lumberjack. There were all sorts: swollen hands, hairy hands, blotchy hands . . .

Mrs. J harvested them with great care, digging around each carrot and pulling gently on the top to extract it, as though the loss of a single finger would have been a great tragedy. Then she would brush away the soil and hold the carrot up in the sunlight to admire it.

"You're terribly stiff," Mrs. J said. I tried to reply, but she had me so completely in her grip that I could manage nothing more than a groan.

I lay down on the bed, as she had instructed, my face buried in a pillow, naked except for a towel around my waist. Then she climbed on my back and pinned me down with tremendous force.

"You sit all day. It's not good for you." She jabbed her thumb into the base of my neck, boring into the flesh.

"Look here, it's knotted up like a ball." I tried to move, to squirm free of the pain, but she had me clamped down tight with her legs, completely immobilized.

Her fingers were cold and hard, and seemed to have no trace of skin or flesh on them. It was as though she were massaging me with her bones.

"We've got to get this loosened up," she said. The bed creaked and the towel began to slide down my hips. Her dentures clattered. I was afraid that if she went on much longer, her fingers would scrape away my skin, rip my flesh, crush my bones. The pillow was damp with saliva, and I wanted to scream.

"That's right. Stand just a little closer together. Now, big smile!"

The reporter's voice echoed through the courtyard as he focused his camera. Perhaps he thought Mrs. J was hard of hearing. "Hold the carrot just a bit higher . . . by the greens so we can see all five fingers. That's it, now don't move."

We were posing right in the middle of the vegetable bed, the reporter trampling on pine needles as he positioned himself for the shot. The other tenants peered curiously from their windows.

I tried to smile, but I couldn't. It was all I could do to keep my eyes open in the blinding sunlight. My mouth, my arms, my eyes—everything seemed to be coming apart and I felt terribly awkward. And thanks to the massage, I hurt all over.

"Pretend you're saying something to each other. Just relax . . . and turn the carrot this way . . . It's all about the carrot!"

Mrs. J had done her best to dress up for the occasion. She had put on lipstick and wrapped a scarf over her head. The hem of her dress came almost to her ankles, and she wore a pair of old-fashioned high heels instead of her usual sandals.

But the scarf only emphasized her narrow face, the lipstick had smeared, and somehow her formal dress and heels seemed to clash with the carrots.

"Make us look good," she told the reporter. "In all my years, I've never once been in the newspaper." She let out a husky laugh, and her smile pinched up the wrinkles around her eyes.

The article ran in the regional section of the paper the next morning: CURIOUS CARROTS! HAND-SHAPED AND FRESH FROM GRANNY'S GARDEN!

Chest thrust forward to compensate for her slight frame, Mrs. J stood, listing a bit to the right as her high heel dug into the earth; and though she had laughed during much of the photo session, in the picture she looked almost frightened. But the carrot cradled in her hands was perfect.

I stood next to her, holding a carrot of my own. In the end, I had managed a smile of sorts, but my eyes looked off in a random direction and I was clearly tense and uncomfortable.

The carrots appeared even stranger in the photograph,

like amputated hands with malignant tumors, dangling in front of us, still warm from the earth.

"Did you ever meet her husband?" the inspector asked.

"No, I just moved into the building," I answered.

"Did she tell you he was dead?" asked another officer.

"Yes, she said he had been drinking and had fallen into the sea and died . . . Or maybe she just said that he was missing. I don't really remember. We weren't really very close . . ."

I glanced out at the courtyard. Mrs. J's apartment was empty. The single curtain fluttered in the window.

"Any little detail could be helpful. Did you notice anything suspicious?" said a young policeman, bending down to meet my gaze. "Anything at all?"

"Suspicious?" I said. "Suspicious . . . Once, in the middle of the night, I saw someone running down through the orchard . . . carrying a heavy box. They took it into the post office, the abandoned one at the bottom of the hill."

The post office was searched and found to contain a mountain of kiwis. But when the fruit was cleared out, it revealed only the mangy body of a cat. Then a backhoe was brought in to turn up the garden, releasing a suffocating odor of pine needles. The tenants at their windows covered their noses.

As the sun fell behind the trees in the orchard, the shovel uncovered a decomposing body in the vegetable patch. The autopsy confirmed that it was Mrs. J's husband and that he had been strangled. Traces of his blood were found on her nightgown.

The hands were missing from the corpse, and they never turned up, even after the whole garden had been searched.

THE LITTLE DUSTMAN

The train was full. Every seat was taken and people were standing between cars. The heater seemed to be broken and my legs were cold.

A dozen or so children in navy blue blazers and berets were sitting in the front of the car. The girls had ribbons around their necks and the boys wore bow ties. The man who seemed to be in charge of the children was absorbed in a thick book, but from time to time he would look up to check on them.

For nearly an hour, we had been waiting there, but the conductor just kept repeating the same announcement over the public address system, that there were mechanical difficulties and it would be some time still before we were moving again.

Although it was spring and the cherry trees along the

track were just beginning to bloom, it had suddenly started to snow. Just a flurry at first, but after a while it showed no sign of letting up, and grew heavier as I watched. In no time at all, everything was blanketed in white.

"I'll be late for Mama's funeral," I murmured to myself. Glancing at my watch, I rubbed the fog from the window. My fingers were cold and wet.

I had learned of Mama's death from my girlfriend, who worked as an editor for an arts-and-crafts magazine.

"That writer, the one you said was your stepmother for a while . . . she died," she told me. "From a heart attack, the day before yesterday. I'm sorry, I probably shouldn't have told you." I could tell she wanted to avoid hurting me.

I had called the woman my mother only from the time I was ten until I turned twelve. Just about the same age as the kids in the front of the train car—and almost thirty years ago now. But it had been the only time in my life that I'd had anything like a real mother.

My biological mother had died shortly after giving birth to me. She had scratched a pimple inside her nose and it had become infected.

"The nose is close to the brain." This had been my father's way of explaining what had happened. "You have to be careful. Germs can get right into the brain through the nose."

Which is why I have always been terrified of going to the ear-nose-and-throat doctor. When they insert that crooked tube in my nose, I can't escape the thought that it will go right through and stick into my brain.

I had no memory of my real mother, no idea what a mother was. Until that woman came to live with us, a mother to me was no more than a metallic sensation in the back of my nose.

My father's new wife was a young woman, just fourteen years older than me, who worked in an art supply shop. He was a middle school art teacher, and it seemed he did a lot of business with the shop.

Mama, as I came to call her, was quiet and petite. Even to the eyes of a child, every feature of her body—neck, fingernails, knees, feet—seemed almost miniature. The first impression I had of her was a pair of tiny shoes I found one day in the entrance hall. They were elegant black high heels, the kind a grown woman wears, but they seemed small enough to fit in the palm of my hand.

Our life as a family got off to an awkward start. We did our best to play the assigned roles—father, mother, son—knowing, though, that if we tried too hard it would never work. It's strange to think about it now, but even a ten-year-old has a certain kind of common sense.

My father gave Mama a cloisonné pendant he had made in his "studio"—a storeroom next to the art class. It was a hexagon hung on a gold chain with flecks of green, violet, deep red, and yellow, the colors changing with the light. It was small, like her, and she almost never took it off.

She was happy when I called her Mama; it made her

feel like a grown-up, she said. So I always called her Mama. Even after they divorced just two years later, she continued to be Mama in my mind.

I was upset, then, a few years later, to discover that I could no longer remember her real name, but I was reluctant to ask my father, who had left no trace of her in his world. So I searched the house, afraid I'd lose all connection to her if I did nothing to conjure her memory. Finally, deep in a drawer, I found the pendant. The colors were as brilliant as ever, and her name was engraved on the back. Relieved, I returned it to the drawer.

Mama had talked very little when we were together during those two years. I could tell she didn't want to bother me. She never cross-examined me or forced a topic of conversation, and when I spoke, she smiled and listened carefully. The rest of the time we were content to keep quiet.

In general, Mama had little to say when other people were present, but when she was alone she talked to herself all the time. I would sneak in to spy on her when she was making dinner or washing dishes, and I would often catch her muttering something under her breath. It sounded a little like singing, or lines from a play, or perhaps she was praying. I never managed to catch what she was saying, and as soon as she realized I was there, she would stop and cover her embarrassment by chopping something or rattling a pan.

When Mama had free time, she would sit at the dining room table and write. She would open a notebook and then fuss with her hair or scrape together a pile of eraser dust for a minute or two. But then her pencil would suddenly start racing across the paper.

"What are you writing?" I would ask. Even when I interrupted her, she never got angry.

"A novel," she always answered. She seemed to actually prefer having me around. She would watch me intently, as though the next word in her story might be hidden somewhere inside me.

"Why are you writing that?"

"Because I want to. That's all. But we aren't going to tell Papa, okay?"

"Why not?"

"Because your father is a real artist."

In fact, I have no idea whether my father was a real artist or not. It's true that he made things in his studio, but it was usually nothing more than a pipe for himself, a pencil box for me, a nameplate for the front door, or a collar for the dog. Mama must have been very impressed by the pendant.

On nights when my father was going to be out late or when he was away on a school trip, Mama would come to my room. After I had changed into my pajamas, she would sit me down on a chair and read to me from her novel.

To tell the truth, I don't remember the story at all. I suppose it must have been much too difficult for a ten-year-old to understand, but that never seemed to bother Mama. She seemed to like her audience of one.

What I do remember is her low, powerful voice, which sounded odd coming from such a tiny body. The pages rustled when she turned them, the pendant swayed gently at her breast.

Even long after my bedtime, she would still be reading, staring at the notebook without looking up. I sat, hands on my knees, trying to look interested. Mama's lips would get dry and cracked, and her voice would go hoarse. Eventually, she started to slur her words, and her voice quivered so much I worried she was about to cry. I would pray for her to stop; I didn't like to see Mama suffering like that.

The woman sitting next to me had taken all sorts of things out of her bag to help pass the time while we waited for the train to start moving again. Postcards, her knitting, some mandarin oranges—objects emerged as if by magic. Now she was busy with a crossword puzzle, and when she came up with an answer, she would excitedly tap the pen on the magazine and scribble in the blanks.

Across from us were two girls who looked like university students. They were simply dressed and wore little makeup; their conversation sounded very serious. In fact, it sounded like an argument of some sort, the kind that goes in circles. One of them would say something and they'd talk about that for a while, and then the other one would say something else and they'd go back to the beginning. They took little notice of the train delay, or of my fidgeting anxiety that I might miss Mama's funeral.

The children in the front of the car were well behaved, sitting quietly and amusing themselves as best they could.

When their teacher began handing out candy, they waited patiently and ate it in silence.

The wind blustered again and the snow swirled outside, covering the woods and grass, the roofs of the farms, the earthen bank along the track.

It was snowing like this the day Mama and I went to the zoo. Mama proposed the outing. I'm writing about a zoo in my next novel and I need to go see one, she'd said. So we went, despite the weather.

The zoo was empty—just Mama and me, and the sour lady at the ticket window. I was wearing a brown coat with artificial fur at the collar and cuffs, earmuffs, gloves, and two pairs of socks. We held hands as we walked, and when a gust of wind came we would huddle close together.

"What animals do you want to see?" I asked.

"Let's see all of them," she said. She looked even tinier and more fragile bundled up against the snow. Her boots were barely big enough for a doll, and her body seemed to vanish into her coat. We walked around the whole zoo, stopping to peer into each cage, but perhaps because of the cold, they were nearly all empty.

Cheetah, Bengal tiger, puma, camel, antelope, lion . . . I read the nameplates as we stood for a moment in front of each cage. Dry leaves floating in a water dish, traces of blood clinging to a bone, droppings scattered about—and the snow piling up on everything.

My only concern was Mama. Was she seeing enough? Had she found what she needed for her story?

Rhinoceros, llama, flamingo, ostrich . . .

Only the penguins and the polar bears were out enjoying themselves. The snow suited them fine. The penguins were busy diving in their pond, while the polar bears paced their cage, thick necks swaying from side to side. The snow glazed their fur with a sparkling crust.

Anteater, sloth, gibbon, cobra, hedgehog, crocodile . . .

Eventually we found we could imagine the animals even without seeing them. The tiger yawning, the llama twitching its ears, the sloth shifting its grip on a branch.

"Why do you suppose giraffes have such long necks?" Mama said, brushing the snow from the railing in front of the cage.

"I don't know," I said.

"It seems absurd, doesn't it?" I nodded vaguely, not quite sure what "absurd" meant. "Long necks that serve no purpose. An elephant uses its trunk to take a shower, an anteater eats with its nose, but a giraffe's neck is useless."

"That's true," I agreed.

"I suppose they learn to live with them somehow, but if I were a giraffe, I'd want a normal neck." She sounded terribly sad.

When we had been around to see every cage, Mama bought us soft-serve ice-cream cones at the snack stand. She took off her gloves in order to dig the coin purse out from the bottom of her bag. Her fingers looked numb as she counted out the change. We sat down to eat them on a bench. It seems ridiculous now that we wanted ice cream on such a cold day, but at the time it felt perfectly natural.

The snow fell on our cones, and we ate it along with the

ice cream, but it didn't have much flavor. Mama looked at me from time to time, and not wanting to disappoint her, I tried to appear as though I were enjoying myself. We could hear the animals howling over the wind.

I wonder whether Mama ever wrote her story about the zoo? In any case, she never read it aloud to me.

"We apologize for the delay. Thank you for your patience." The announcement played over and over, and was greeted by sighs up and down the car.

"'A shooting star with a long tail.' What could that be?" said the woman next to me, tapping her pen against her temple.

"Comet?" I suggested.

"It's six letters," she said, counting "c . . . o . . . m . . . e . . . t" under her breath.

"Meteor," said one of the college students across from us.

"M . . . e . . . t . . . e . . . o . . . r. That's it. It fits perfectly. Thank you." She eagerly filled in the blanks.

"Not at all," said the girl, turning back to her conversation.

It was difficult for me to believe that Mama had grown old. In my memory she was unchanged from that day at the zoo, and younger than I am now. When I finally arrive at the funeral and see her picture on the altar, will I feel that I am looking at a total stranger?

"It says her body was discovered by the paper boy," my girlfriend had said. "He thought it was strange that no one answered the door even though he could hear the TV. She was found with her head resting on her desk, as though she'd been writing something."

"Did she have a heart condition?" I asked.

"It doesn't say. But she hadn't published much in almost ten years, so none of our editors had ever met her. But . . ." She hesitated.

"Tell me what it says," I prompted. "I want to know."

"She apparently had psychological problems brought on by writer's block. She thought her work was being plagiarized, or that someone was coming in and taking things when she was away from home. She made quite a fuss about it, and she apparently started carrying her manuscripts around tied up in a scarf."

Mama was not a particularly successful writer. About five or six years after the divorce, I happened to see a short piece in the newspaper saying that she had won a new writer's prize. I bought the book and read it. It was a strange story about an old lady who owns an apartment building and grows carrots in the courtyard. She digs up one in the shape of a human hand, with five perfect fingers. In the end, they discover her husband's body buried in the garden, minus the hands. That was the general idea.

She had several books published after she won the prize, but no one took much notice. I would find them in the remainders bin; when I brought them home, I had to hide them from my father.

"Well then . . ." said the man, clearing his throat. The children stood up and formed two lines in the aisle, their legs apart and their hands behind their backs. The passengers sat watching them; the woman next to me closed her magazine and the college girls fell silent.

"'The Little Dustman' by Johannes Brahms," the man announced, holding up a pen for a conductor's baton.

The voices of the children reverberated above our heads, voices almost too beautiful to be human, rippling the surface of memory. I prayed for Mama as the snow continued to fall.

Later, someone sent me a small box of things she had left behind. A few trinkets, some clothing, fragments of manuscripts—and a faded picture clipped from a newspaper that had been tucked into the box. In the picture, an emaciated old woman in a headscarf stood smiling in the courtyard of an apartment building. She was holding a carrot in the shape of a hand. Mama was standing next to her, holding a carrot, too, and looking terribly uncomfortable. It had been a beautiful day and Mama was squinting in the sunlight.

I have no idea why Mama left us. Toward the end, she talked to herself more and more, and she no longer bothered to stop even when she realized I was in the room. She muttered almost constantly, like a broken record. At some point I realized the pendant had disappeared from around her neck.

On her last day with us, she held my cheeks in her hands. "You've been a good boy," she said. "I wish that I was so good." Her hands were as cold as they had been on that snowy day at the zoo.

LAB COATS

"Nephrology, one short. Endocrinology, one long. Emergency Room, one short."

I take a lab coat from the mountain of dirty ones on the floor and I check the pockets. I read out the size and the name of the department written in magic marker on the back of the collar and then toss it in the cart. She sits next to me, writing down each coat in the register, so that next week, when they come back from the laundry, we can check them against the list to be sure nothing's missing. Of all the jobs we secretaries at the hospital have to do, this is the one we hate the most. Partly because it's nasty and boring, but also because the laundry room is next to the morgue.

She and I take an old freight elevator to the basement—just a cold, rattling box, really—and then walk down this long hall that's so tight I don't see how they roll the gurneys through. The walls are scuffed up, and the fluorescent light flickers creepily. The floor of the hall slopes down from the elevator, so the laundry cart rolls forward on its own, as though pulled by an invisible hand. Like it's going to race down the hall and crash through the door of the morgue. That's creepy, too.

To be honest, the morgue doesn't scare me much. I don't really understand why the other girls are so afraid of it. They see people dying all over the hospital, while they type their reports or eat cream puffs in the lounge. The job is even kind of nice, especially when she's next to me. She's as beautiful underground as she is in the office, her face all white and pale.

"Dermatology, two short. Cardiology, one long. Oral Surgery, one short . . ." No matter how long we work, the mountain never seems to get any smaller.

"He should be in the endo lab this afternoon," she says, without looking up. Endoscopy.

"Right," I agree, "it's Monday." I know the whole schedule by heart. "I can manage here if you want to go."

"No," she says, running her finger down the list to Oral Surgery. "No need."

Her boyfriend is a resident in Respiratory Medicine, and right about now he's probably putting an endoscope down someone's throat.

I pick up the next coat, turn it inside out, and shake it. Something falls out of the pocket and rolls across the floor: a dried-up plum. Looks like a testicle.

I've given up trying to figure out how this stuff gets in their pockets. And this isn't even the weirdest thing; I've seen flower bulbs, bras, corks, a Bible, a little eggplant, condoms—you name it.

"He was supposed to come see me last night, but he never showed up," she says.

"Maybe one of his patients took a turn for the worse," I say, tossing the plum in the trash.

"He went to see his in-laws to tell them about the divorce; he said he'd come and tell me how it went." The doctor's wife went home to her family last month to give birth to their third child—first girl. I knew all the details. "He was full of excuses again. Something about the train getting stuck in snow. He claimed he never even got there, that he sat on the train the whole time and had to come back without seeing them. Can you believe the nerve? He expects me to believe a story like that with the cherry trees already in bloom."

"I don't know," I say. "He could be telling the truth. Freak snowstorms happen. You should check the weather report. If he was going to lie to you, he would have said it was a patient." She doesn't seem to be listening.

Since the day I started my job at the hospital, I've always enjoyed working with her. She's a hard worker and she doesn't take grief from the doctors or anyone else. And she's beautiful. I never get tired of looking at her. It must be nice being that pretty.

I especially like to watch her work—the way her eyes light up in front of the computer screen, that cute little ear that sticks out from under her hair when she answers the phone. But best of all is her tongue when she's licking those blue airmail envelopes. It flicks out, all moist and red, and runs over the gluey edge.

"I wouldn't mind having a peek down one of those scopes," I say, just to make conversation. She nods, but she's still not listening.

The next coat has bloodstains. I wonder whether the patient suffered much—before I toss it in the cart.

"They used one on me when I was a kid," I add. "A peanut went down the wrong tube and I couldn't breathe. Nearly suffocated. It's weird that one peanut could kill you."

She doesn't answer, so I go back to reading labels. The room smells like death and disinfectant.

The two of them have been doing it all over the hospital—in the wards, the labs, the broom closet. Maybe he's even put the endoscope down her throat. Bet she looks as good inside as out—warm, red, inviting, all those little wrinkles tempting you deeper and deeper . . .

She knows exactly how she wants a job to be done. Twenty pages or fewer gets a paper clip; more than twenty, a binder clip. Sugar packets are for staff meetings; sugar cubes for guests. The surgery schedule is expected to be blown up 150 percent, and copies posted on the bulletin board (upper left-hand corner), on the side of the equipment locker, and on the door to the lounge. If a patient gives you cookies or other food, it goes on the middle shelf in the cupboard.

Not long after I started working here, some bigwig in Neurology asked us to help with a presentation he was going to give at a conference. It had all these graphs and charts, and he wanted it back in just two days. She split the work with me and we typed up labels for the slides.

"Use the number 508 stickers for the slides," she told me. "They're for conferences." No. 508 was a dull gray.

I did the job just the way she had asked, but when the doctor returned to pick up the presentation, he took one look at it and threw it back on the desk. It all tumbled down onto the floor.

"This color won't show up on the projector," he said.

"I'm terribly sorry," she said, stepping in before I had the chance to say anything. Her apology was really smooth. "I told her to use number 608 as usual, but it's my fault for not checking. She's new and I think she's a little color-blind. I'm very sorry. We'll get it redone by the end of the day."

The doctor said he'd be back later and stormed out.

Color-blind? For a moment I wasn't sure what she'd said—just that she'd sounded really charming when she'd said it. No. 608 was bright blue.

She had definitely told me no. 508. I knew because it was the same number as her apartment. I wasn't likely to make a mistake about something like that. And she had given the presentation one more pass before the doctor had come to get it. I started picking up the papers.

"It's your mistake," she said. "You fix it."

I didn't finish until way after midnight. I felt like I was sinking in some kind of gray swamp.

The next morning she handed the new slides to the

doctor as if she'd done them herself. He seemed really embarrassed he'd made such a fuss and he asked her out to lunch to apologize. I was not invited.

I never said a word of what happened, not to anyone. I was willing to be color-blind if it would keep her perfect.

"I told you she got pregnant just when he was about to ask her for the divorce." I shake the next coat and two cafeteria tickets fall out of the pocket: one for spaghetti with meatballs and one for a cream soda. "I bet she did it on purpose, part of her evil scheme."

She isn't looking at me, but she doesn't seem to be writing in the register anymore either. She's usually such a perfectionist, but she can get pretty sloppy if she's thinking about her doctor.

"When I asked him if he'd even told her, he got defensive and came up with all these excuses: they're worried about the boy getting into the right elementary school; his wife could go into premature labor; he's got some experiment running at the lab and can't be distracted; the train got stuck in the snow . . . a load of crap!"

She stops for a moment and I read the label on the next coat. She writes it down in the register—I think.

The coats are in a pretty sorry state, all wrinkled and stained. Blood, spit, urine, tears. You can tell by the color, and the smell. It's amazing all the stuff that can ooze out of a body.

"'One lie leads to another,'" I say. She should know.

"He finally showed up past ten last night. Dog-tired—

from being stuck on the train for five hours, he said. But I was the one who was tired. Tired of waiting all that time, of running to the door at every little noise, watching the dinner I'd made get cold."

She runs her hand through her hair and looks down again. Her skin is so white. Her shoulders are really beautiful. The pen rolls across the desk.

"Do you know what he told me? He said he'd 'had a lot of time to think' on the train. That he felt like 'some invisible force' was holding him back. That it 'wasn't the right time,' and that was why it had snowed. He said he wanted me to be patient, to wait just a little longer. 'Just a little longer . . .' And then we screwed, just like we always do. That's all we have left."

I imagine her naked. The doctor's fingers running over her skin, her hair, the wet places. I picture her tongue licking the edge of the blue envelope. Who wouldn't want her?

"Gastrointestinal Med., two long. Ophthalmology, one short. Neurosurgery, one long. Pediatrics, four short." I pick up the pace, trying to distract her, but she's not paying attention anymore. The pen's still on the desk.

"How could he be so cruel? How could he tell me to wait? No, I couldn't wait any longer. Not one more day, not one more second."

I take the register and begin checking in the coats myself, trying to be as neat as she is.

"That's why I killed him," she says. Her voice is low and cold.

I feel a scream rising out of me, but somehow I stop it, hold it back, and instead I calmly imagine the scene: the knife in her pretty hand; the blade slicing into him again and again; skin ripping, blood spurting. But she's spotless. I pick up the next coat.

"Respiratory Medicine, one long."

It's his. I shake it and out falls a tongue. It's still soft. Maybe even warm.

SEWING FOR THE HEART

"Dr. Y from Respiratory Medicine. Dr. Y from Respiratory Medicine. Please contact the pharmacy immediately."

The public address system had been repeating this announcement for some time. I wondered who Dr. Y was and where he could be, as I studied the hospital directory. Central Records, Electro-Shock Clinic, Conference Center, Endoscopy . . . It was all like a foreign language to me.

"Why do they keep paging this Dr. Y?" I asked the woman behind the information desk.

"No one's seen him this morning," she said. She seemed annoyed by my question, and I was sorry I had bothered her.

"Could you tell me where to find the cardiac ward," I said, getting to my real question. I pronounced each word slowly and carefully, hoping to quiet the pounding of my heart.

"Take that elevator to the sixth floor." She pointed past a crowd of people gathered in front of Admitting; I noticed her nail polish was chipped.

I am a bag maker. For more than twenty years now I've kept a shop near the train station. It's just a small place, but it has a nice display window facing the street. Inside, there are tables for the bags and a mirror, and a workshop in back, behind a curtain, with shelves for my materials. The window features a few purses, an ostrich handbag, and a suitcase. A jauntily posed mannequin clutches one of the purses, but her face is covered in a fine layer of dust because I haven't changed the window in years.

I live on the second floor, above the shop. My apartment has just two rooms—an eat-in kitchen and a living room that doubles as my bedroom—but the place is bright and pleasant. On clear afternoons the sun streams in through the window and I have to move the hamster's cage under the washstand. Hamsters don't like direct sunlight.

In the evening, after closing shop, I go upstairs, take off my work clothes, shower, and eat my dinner. This takes next to no time. When you live alone as I have for many years, daily life only becomes simpler and simpler. It's been a long time since I've cleaned up the bathroom for someone, or changed the towels, or so much as made dressing for my salad. I have only myself to please, and that doesn't take much.

But compared with the world upstairs, my life with my

bags below is quite rich. I never weary of them, of caressing and gazing at my wonderful creations. When I make a bag, I begin by picturing how it will look when it's finished. Then I sketch each imagined detail, from the shiny clasp to the finest stitches in the seams. Next, I transfer the design to pattern paper and cut out the pieces from the raw material, and then finally I sew them together. As the bag begins to take shape on my table, my heart beats uncontrollably and I feel as though my hands wield all the powers of the universe.

Now, you may be wondering why I get so excited. You may be thinking that a bag is just a thing in which to put other things. And you're right, of course. But that's what makes them so extraordinary. A bag has no intentions or desires of its own, it embraces every object that we ask it to hold. You trust the bag, and it, in return, trusts you. To me, a bag is patience; a bag is profound discretion.

So then, in the evenings, when I've finished my dinner, I sit on the couch by the window and drink a cup of Chinese tea. I turn off the lamp in the room and look down on the street below. The passersby are cast in a seductive shadow. People drift by under my window—strolling couples, men returning late from the office, women from the bars, drunks—and all of them are carrying bags. Here's a filthy one with two long scratches on the side. That puffy one seems to mimic the face of its owner. That one's cracked and faded, as though it was left out in the rain. In the moonlight I see these details, savor them for a few seconds as they pass below my window.

As I sit and watch the bags, the hamster runs on his

treadmill. Hamsters are nocturnal, so he seems to wake up when I turn off the lamp. From time to time he makes a tiny sneezing noise, but nothing more.

A woman with a shoulder bag passes by. Her hips twist and the bag turns toward me, revealing a clasp on the front. The strap cuts into the material of her blouse. Next comes a woman carrying a Boston bag. She holds the handle so tightly, it seems her fingers might leave a deep impression on the leather. There must be something very important inside.

The hamster stuffs his cheeks with sunflower seeds. I take a sip of tea. My hands ache from a long day of gripping the needle and the awl.

I can make any kind of bag a customer wants: bags for artificial limbs, bedpans, rifles, eggs, dentures—any size and shape you can imagine. But I have to admit I hesitated when she told me her request, one I had never heard before and I'm sure I'll never hear again.

"I would like you to make a bag to hold a heart."

"A heart?" I blurted out, thinking I must have misunderstood. Then I coughed to cover my confusion and offered her a seat. She slipped off her coat and hung it over the back of the chair before sitting down. The coat was too heavy for the season and a bit too big. Her movements were graceful, but they seemed calculated somehow, almost intentionally seductive.

"A heart—" I began again.

"I was told you could make any kind of bag." She took

off her sunglasses and tapped the table with her long fingernails.

"I can," I said, slowly opening my sketchbook as I struggled to collect myself. "And you want a bag for a heart?"

"That's right," she said. Her voice had an impressive coldness to it—I could almost imagine its tone freezing my eardrum.

She was tall and slender with gently sloping shoulders—all wrong for a shoulder strap. Her hair was curly and long in back. She kept her eyes lowered, but her manner was anything but timid.

There was a moment of awkward silence. Something about her had set my nerves jangling, even before she had uttered her request. Perhaps it was the crocodile purse on her lap. It was a beautiful piece of work, but it was stretched out of shape and the leather had lost its luster—probably from improper cleaning. It seemed weary. Customers who come here to order new bags naturally bring their old ones with them, and they tell me a lot about the people carrying them.

"A number of places have turned me away," she said, taking me into her confidence. She brushed a wisp of hair away from her eyes and turned to look at the row of samples on the shelf.

It was then that I realized I had been bothered not by her purse but by the unnatural bulge on the left side of her chest. It was clearly not her breast; the swell of a breast is different. This looked more like a tumor that had grown between her collarbone and her armpit, unbalancing her natural symmetry. But it wasn't a tumor.

"I've tried everything," she said. "Silk, cotton, nylon, vinyl, paper . . . nothing is right. It has to be kept warm—heat loss can be fatal—but then there are the secretions. If the material is too absorbent, it sucks up all the moisture. But then again, something like vinyl doesn't breathe."

She had explained that she was born with her heart outside her chest—as difficult as that might be to imagine. It worked normally enough, but its unique location made it extremely vulnerable. She had to avoid bumping it or exposing it to the air, yet still keep it supported next to her body. Strictly speaking, it wasn't a "bag" she wanted—at least not like any I'd made in the past—but she was a customer, and I was determined to do my best to satisfy her.

"I think seal skin would be ideal," I said, going to the shelf to get a sample. "It's soft and strong, and it repels moisture while providing superior insulation—just what a seal needs. And it's easy to care for."

"It sounds perfect," she said, taking the piece of leather. She stroked the surface, turned it over, crumpled it in her hand. "But I'm afraid the shape will be a bit complicated, like a bra for just one side. It has to be very sturdy but still not damage the membrane. Do you understand?"

"I believe so. Just tell me exactly what you want," I said, starting to sketch in my book. In fact, I had no idea what I was trying to draw, but I didn't want to disappoint her.

"It needs to have a snug fit. Too loose and it rubs the

sack around the heart, but if it's too tight, it cuts off the circulation. It's a matter of striking the right balance."

"Exactly so," I said. "But that's true for any bag, and I think you'll find my work to your satisfaction."

"I hope so," she said, and then she smiled for the first time since coming into the shop. She crossed her legs and sat back, fidgeting with the temples of her sunglasses. Her subtlest movements caused the lump on her chest to shift, as though she had stirred a small, slumbering animal. I noticed that she kept her left arm cradled next to her body to protect the heart; no doubt she wore the heavy coat for the same reason.

"But it's not just a simple sack," she continued. "You'll need holes for the veins and arteries. I suppose you should baste it together first to make sure everything matches up. And it needs a strap to hang around my neck."

It occurred to me then that I would have to see her exposed heart at some point in the process—a prospect that disturbed me. I had never seen a human heart before, and the thought filled me with fear and disgust.

The woman removed her blouse and bra without a moment's hesitation, as though I weren't even there. I had led her upstairs to my apartment and had drawn the curtains. The hamster's cage had been stored under the sink; he was sleeping peacefully.

I was shocked to see the heart beating—for some reason, I had imagined it would be inanimate. But there it was, pulsing and contracting. It seemed to cringe under my gaze. Then there was the blood flowing in the vessels. It was clear, not red, pumping through the fine veins and arteries and then disappearing into her body.

Her left breast hung lower than her right, and there was a slight hollowing above it to accommodate the heart. But the skin was firm, like that of a younger woman, and the nipple was perfectly normal. It seemed odd to be looking at a woman's breast but feeling no desire to touch it, or to take the nipple between my lips. Instead, I found myself longing to caress her heart.

It could fit in the palm of my hand. A pale pink membrane of delicate muscle tissue surrounded it. What extraordinary, breathtaking beauty! Would it feel damp if I cupped it in my hands? Would the membrane rupture if I gave it a squeeze? Could I feel it beating? Feel it shrink from my caresses? I wanted to run my fingertips over each tiny bump and furrow, touch my lips to the veins, soft tissue on soft tissue, the pressure of her pulse against my skin . . . I could easily lose myself to these thoughts, but I knew I had to keep this desire in check, had to play my role and make the perfect bag for this heart.

"Let me wash my hands first," I said, trying to keep my voice from trembling.

"Please do." Her tone was impassive.

The hamster stirred, startled by the sound of my footsteps coming to the sink, but then he fell silent again.

I washed my hands with great care. Like a surgeon in a TV drama, I lathered the soap and scrubbed right up to my elbows, then used a brush on my nails and cuticles. But when I went and stood in front of her, I found myself paralyzed, unsure where to begin.

The woman stood, back straight, arms at her side. The slope of her shoulders was even more pronounced now that they were bare; it was most likely due to the cavity in her chest, which had caused her rib cage to contract. She had a mole on her right shoulder, and her collarbones jutted sharply above her breasts. There was no excess fat anywhere on her body. . . . I allowed all of this to distract me from looking at her heart, even though it was directly in front of my eyes. The desire was overwhelming.

As I stepped closer to her, I sensed that I had somehow shrunk in her presence. Then I pulled out my tape and started taking measurements. Its shape was complicated, and it was a long process. I had to delicately measure the diameter of each vein and artery, the subtle tapering of the ventricles, and every centimeter of its beating surface. I worked with great care to avoid any more contact with the heart than was necessary. What if the measuring tape stuck to the viscous membrane, or if germs passed from my hands to the vulnerable organ? I was a mass of anxieties.

"You needn't be so timid," she told me. "It's tougher than it looks." She must have sensed what I was feeling. It was unlikely she had allowed many strangers this view of her heart, yet she seemed perfectly comfortable with the situation and not the least bit wary or embarrassed.

But the heart itself still appeared to be cowering in fear, the blood vessels trembling with each contraction. From close up, the sinews and folds of muscle seemed to conceal a mysterious code.

Then my finger accidentally brushed against it.

It was so warm! Warmer than anything I had ever touched before. The heat shot through my hand, filling my body and emptying my head.

The measuring tape dropped at my feet.

"I'm sorry," I muttered. I gathered up the tape as she stood over me. My fingertip was still tingling. I could hear the hamster sucking at his water bottle.

I learned she was a singer, and that she performed regularly at a club nearby. After I had stitched together a sample of the bag for her heart, I went in secret to hear her sing. It was the first time I had ever gone to see a customer outside my shop. In fact, even in the shop I tend to have no more to do with them than is absolutely necessary. I feel that my connection to them should be solely through my bags. So if I had to explain why I made an exception in this case, I would say that I had no particular interest in the woman herself, but that I simply wanted to see her heart in the outside world.

The club was larger and quieter than I had thought it would be, which I hoped would allow me to spy on her without being recognized. Alcohol and tobacco stains had darkened the wood of the candlelit tables scattered around the room; the floor was littered with peanut shells. The woman stood next to a grand piano in a circle of orange light at the front of the room.

She was wearing a long, tight purple dress made of silky material. And over it was a sequined cape that sparkled in the spotlight—a clever disguise for the lump on her chest. Still, she probably would have preferred something more stylish; the cape reminded me a bit of a nun's habit.

I sat down at a table in the corner and ordered a beer. It hardly mattered what I ordered, since I can't drink alcohol. The waiter put a bowl of peanuts on the table and left.

The people at the other tables were drinking quietly. No one seemed to be looking at her, though I suspected that some of them must have been aware of her secret.

She began to sing, but I could not make out the words. It must have been a love song, to judge from the slightly pained expression on her face, and the way she tightly gripped the microphone. I noticed a flash of white skin on her neck. As she reached the climax of the song, her eyes half closed and her shoulders thrown back, a shudder passed through her body. She moved her arm across her chest to cradle her heart, as though consoling it, afraid it might burst. I wondered what would happen if I held her tight in my arms, in a lovers' embrace, melting into one another, bone on bone . . . her heart would be crushed. The membrane would split, the veins tear free, the heart itself explode into bits of flesh, and then my desire would contain hers—it was all so painful and yet so utterly beautiful to imagine.

The song ended, and like everyone else in the club, I applauded.

When she bowed, I worried gravity would pull her heart from her dress. But almost immediately, she began another song.

The day arrived for the first fitting of the bag. The weather was sunny and mild, but she appeared in a heavy coat just as she had when she first came to see me.

The room was warm, even with the curtains closed. The hamster had left his nest and was sleeping on the wire floor of the cage. Though he normally slept in a ball, today he was stretched out full-length.

The woman's chest was dripping with sweat, but that made the skin glow whiter than ever.

"Tell me if it hurts you in any way," I said. She nodded but said nothing.

It was indeed a strange bag. The complicated shape of it was difficult to achieve. I had assembled nine different pieces of leather into an asymmetrical balloon with seven holes of varying size. The bottom of it was an oval, but the bag tapered toward an opening at the top that fastened with hooks. The strap for her neck was long and somewhat awkward, as the leather hadn't had time to soften. I was afraid she might get tangled in it.

It looked like a spider, or a work of modern art. Or a fetus that had just started to grow.

I undid the hooks. Even before I touched the heart, my fingers could feel the heat; it made my head spin and my palms sweat.

"Hurry up," she said, sounding irritated.

"Yes, of course," I answered, fastening the hooks as quickly as I could. "I'm sorry. Shall I attach the strap as well?"

"Please do," she said. Her arms hung at her sides, and she made no effort to look at the bag. My hand passed through her hair and fastened the strap around her neck. I took a step back and wiped my palms on the front of my apron. Then I took a deep breath.

The bag suited her to perfection. The lustrous finish of the leather set off the color of her skin, and its shape fit elegantly along the curve of her breast. The veins and arteries peeking out at the edges, the leather pulsing almost imperceptibly with each contraction, the strap caressing her graceful neck—I had never seen anything like it.

Her blouse and slip were discarded on the couch. The loudspeaker at the train station droned softly in the distance. I stood and admired my handiwork.

"The hole for the artery here is too high," she said, shrugging her shoulders. "Please fix it."

"Of course," I said. "I'll make the adjustment."

The bag conformed to her every movement, protecting her heart like a faithful servant.

"It is nice and light," she continued, "but the hooks rub my side."

"I'll use smaller ones and move them around to the front."

"Yes, that might help." She continued to test the fit—loosening the strap, rolling her shoulders, and finally striking a pose as though a microphone were in her hand.

"What's that?" she said, pointing at a little bag sitting on the shelf above the sink.

"It's for the hamster," I said as I refilled her teacup.

"The hamster?"

We had removed her heart from the bag and she was buttoning up her blouse.

"I put him in it when I take him out for a walk. He seems to enjoy it."

"Did you make his bag, too?"

"Of course."

She stared curiously at the pouch: a simple thing compared with hers, with nothing more than a few air holes in the side.

"I never knew there were so many different kinds of bags," she said.

I took a sip of tea and looked out at the bright sunlight.

The bag was almost finished. The leather was a soft cream color, the cutting and stitching were precise down to the millimeter. I had hung a sign on the door announcing that the shop would be closed until further notice and had spent long hours at my worktable. A regular customer had even called to ask me to repair her makeup case, but I turned her away.

The beauty of the heart oppressed me, but my hands were steady as I worked. I had managed to make a thing that no one else could have made.

The hamster died. It might have been the heat wave, or maybe I neglected him because I was so absorbed in my work. I fed him and cleaned his cage every other day—for three years and eight months—but he died anyway.

He lay still in my hand, teeth sticking out from his half-opened mouth. His body was still soft, but he already felt cold to the touch. I had no idea what to do with him, so I put him in his pouch, left my apartment, and wandered the streets of the town. I walked along the banks of the river, through the park, and around the reservoir, but I couldn't find a place to get rid of him. From time to time I stopped to unzip the pouch and check on him, but he was definitely dead.

When I got tired of walking, I stopped in at a hamburger place. I didn't really want a hamburger, but it was too much trouble to find a real restaurant.

I could barely eat half the food on my plate, and the coffee was almost undrinkable. When I went to throw away the trash, I slipped the hamster out of the pouch, on the tray next to my food, and slid him in the bin. I don't think anyone noticed.

He must be covered in ketchup by now.

"What do you mean?" I asked her.

"Just what I said. I won't be needing the bag." She took a cigarette from her purse and lit it.

"But it will be done in a day or two . . ."

"I know it seems absurd to cancel the order at this point, and you have every right to be angry. But it all happened so suddenly—I can hardly believe it myself." She let out a puff of smoke, and I watched it float toward the ceiling.

"I've known for some time that it might be possible to put my heart back in place, but the operation always seemed too risky. Then I found a marvelous surgeon who told me he could do it using a new technique." She went on like this a while longer, but I wasn't listening.

"I'll be going into the hospital next week, and I'll be rid of this depressing thing forever." She glanced down at her side with a look that was almost scornful.

"But it's a wonderful bag. Here, see for yourself. I've moved the hole for the artery and switched to smaller hooks. I'm sure you'll like it." I held it out for her to see. "I just want to reinforce the stitching here and adjust the strap and it will be done."

"I'll pay you for it, of course. But I won't be needing it now. I won't have anything to put in it."

"But see how exquisite it is. You won't find a bag like this anywhere else. The insulation, the breathability, the quality of the materials, the workmanship . . ."

"I said I won't be needing it." As she stood to go, she brushed the bag from the table and it lay there on the floor, as still as a dead animal.

"Dr. Y from Respiratory Medicine. Dr. Y from Respiratory Medicine. Please contact the pharmacy immediately." The announcement played again, but Dr. Y was apparently still missing.

The elevator was crowded with doctors and nurses, and patients with drip bags of yellow liquid, but I forced my way in and pressed the button for the sixth floor. I was sure I'd be able to find her room. I would pretend I was just visiting her, or I could say I wanted her to pay me for the bag. After all, I ought to get something for all my work.

First, I'll apologize for the other day—very humbly, in order to regain her trust. And then I'll say what I've come to say: "Making your bag has been a very important experience for me. I don't think I'll ever have the chance to make a piece like this again. Still, I'm happy you're getting the operation and won't need the bag. But I do have one final request: I'd like to see it put to its intended use just once. I know it's asking a lot, but I'd be very grateful. I promise I'll never bother you again, but nothing is more painful for a craftsman than knowing all his hard work was for nothing. Just this once, and I'd be eternally grateful."

She'll take off her gown, and I'll fit it on her.

"Are you satisfied, then?" she'll ask, eager to be rid of me.

"Thank you," I'll say, but when I reach for the bag, I'll cut her heart away, too.

And then it will be mine alone.

The bag is in my left pocket. I tried to fold it flat, but there's a little mound in my pants. I don't think anyone will notice. The shears in my right pocket prick my thigh as I wait.

The elevator chimes, the number six lights up, and the door opens.

WELCOME TO THE MUSEUM OF TORTURE

Lots of people died today. In a city to the north, a tour bus tumbled off a cliff, killing twenty-seven and badly injuring six more. A family of three, weighed down with debt, committed suicide by turning on the gas—and when the house exploded, six more died next door. An eighty-six-year-old man was killed by a hit-and-run driver; a child drowned in an irrigation ditch; a fishing boat capsized; some mountain climbers were swept away by an avalanche. There was a flood in China, a plane crash in Nepal, and in Niger a religious cult committed mass suicide.

But it wasn't just humans. I saw a dead hamster in the garbage can at a fast-food place this morning. I was throwing out a coffee cup when I happened to notice it. The can was so full that the lid was half open—a perfectly ordinary sight yet something caught my attention.

A hamster lay between a crumpled hamburger wrapper

and a crushed paper cup. Its fur was speckled brown, and its tiny arms and legs were a beautiful shade of pale pink. The poor thing almost still looked alive. I even imagined I saw its little paws twitching. Its black eyes seemed to be looking at me.

I opened the lid the rest of the way, releasing the smell of ketchup and pickles and coffee all mixed together. I was right, the hamster was moving: hundreds of maggots were worming into its soft belly.

Why was everyone dying? They had all been so alive just yesterday.

A man was murdered in the apartment directly above mine, in number 508. He was apparently doing a residency at the university hospital. He was stabbed more than a dozen times in the neck. They say he was nearly decapitated.

"Did you know him?"

As the detective took the photograph out of his pocket, I pulled back instinctively. I would never be able to eat my dinner after looking at a picture of a bloody, severed head—and I had been just about to add the crushed tomatoes to my minestrone when the doorbell rang.

"Don't worry." The detective's tone was kindly, and the picture turned out to be an ordinary snapshot taken in an office somewhere. There was no blood, and the man's head was squarely on his shoulders.

"No, I've never seen him," I said after examining the photo.

"Do you know anything about the woman who lives upstairs?" The detective was well built, but he seemed very young and quite nervous. I wondered whether it was because he had been looking at a dead body just moments ago—smelling it, maybe even touching it. He appeared to be on edge, almost as if he had committed a murder himself. He kept his head down, and he seemed uncomfortable as he took his notes.

"No, I didn't see her much. Just the occasional 'hello' in the elevator."

"Did you notice men coming and going to her apartment?"

"I'm not sure. I suppose I've seen her with a man, but I don't remember whether it was the one in the picture."

I took another look at the photograph. The man was wearing a white lab coat with a fountain pen and a pair of scissors and a penlight in the breast pocket. He had a stethoscope around his neck. There were wrinkles at the corners of his mouth from the effort of smiling.

"Did you hear any suspicious noises at about eleven o'clock two nights ago?" He spoke each word so distinctly that he was almost stammering.

"I certainly did."

"What kind of noises?" For the first time since the beginning of the interview, he looked me straight in the eyes. I could see he was genuinely interested now.

"It sounded like something heavy being dragged across the floor. I thought she was rearranging the furniture."

"And what time was that?"

"I was brushing my teeth before bed, so it must have been a little past eleven."

"About how long did it last?"

"Just a few seconds. So I didn't think anything of it."

"Did you hear anything that sounded like an argument, any screams?"

"No, nothing like that."

The detective listened to me with his full attention, as though afraid of missing any little detail, and then he scribbled everything down in his notebook. Even though we had just met, I felt I was already indispensable to him.

"By the way, a patient at the university hospital was stabbed to death the other day as well. We're trying to figure out whether there's any connection between the two incidents. Would you know anything at all about that?" He took a second photograph from his pocket.

The woman in the picture appeared to be singing in a bar. She was thirtyish, slender, with a pointy chin and a pout. She had split ends and the roots of her dye job were showing. As a hairdresser, I notice these things.

"The attacker used scissors to gouge a hole in her chest."

"How awful! One in the throat and the other in the heart." I could hear the minestrone bubbling in the kitchen. My apron was splattered with juice from the tomatoes. "No, I've never seen her either," I told him.

"No?" he murmured, clearly disappointed. I felt as though I'd let him down. "The tiniest detail could be helpful. If anything at all comes to mind, don't hesitate to call." I wanted so much to be useful, to say something that would keep him interested. But nothing came to mind. "Well then," he said, bowing politely, "if you think of anything, please get in touch."

"Of course," I said.

My boyfriend arrived just on time. It had been a while since we'd spent our day off together. In fact, we'd been so busy I hadn't seen him in almost three weeks.

We were planning to watch a video and have a quiet dinner at home. Then we might go out to a bookstore or record shop, or take a walk in the park. Or maybe I would cut his hair on the balcony—though he always says it embarrasses him to be seen like that by people in the neighborhood.

Dinner was almost ready. I had seasoned the shrimp, and they just needed to be grilled. The salad was in the refrigerator, and the wineglasses sparkled. The minestrone had boiled a bit too long, but it would still taste fine. I had bought his favorite strawberry shortcake at the bakery on the plaza, and set the table with the new cloth and napkins. Everything was perfect.

"I've been dying to see you," he said as he took me in his arms. Or at least that's what I think he said. His voice was muffled by my hair, and I couldn't hear him clearly, but I decided not to ask him to repeat himself, in case it had been something less romantic.

He took off his coat, inhaled deeply the smell of dinner coming from the kitchen, and pushed back his bangs, which were too long. We sat down on the sofa and held each other, neither of us saying much. We both knew that silence was the best way to appreciate a moment we'd been waiting three weeks for.

I could tell someone was in the apartment upstairs and wondered if the police had come back. It was noisy outside as well, but not enough to disturb our peace. His arm was around my shoulder, and his other hand held mine where it rested in my lap. I laid my cheek against his chest, and I could hear his heart beating, feel his breath on my neck.

When I'm curled up in his arms like this, I can never tell how my body looks to him. I worry that I seem completely ridiculous, but I have the ability to squeeze into any little space he leaves for me. I fold my legs until they take up almost no room at all, and curl in my shoulders until they're practically dislocated. Like a mummy in a tomb. And when I get like this, I don't care if I never get out; or maybe that's exactly what I hope will happen.

Still, the moment came when I had to pull myself away and break the silence.

"Did you know there was a murder upstairs?" I said. For some reason, I couldn't resist telling him. A murder was special, interesting.

"I saw a patrol car parked outside," he said, his hand still holding mine.

"The police were swarming all over the building, and there were lots of reporters. It was awful. They even came here asking questions. I was a nervous wreck—the first time I'd ever talked to a detective in my entire life. Have you ever talked to one?"

He shook his head.

"He was nice enough," I continued. "Seemed new to the

job, but he was very polite. I heard some strange noises the other night, the sound of something heavy being dragged across the floor. Probably had something to do with the murder. He was very interested—about the noises. I didn't think anything of it at the time, but for some reason I remembered. And I had even checked the time without realizing it. It was ten after eleven. Which is really the point. The exact time of death is always important in things like this."

This time he nodded, and I continued.

"They said the victim was a doctor at the university hospital, that he was stabbed to death by his mistress, almost decapitated, actually. It's too horrible to think about. But it's an old story: blind love and jealousy. Though I don't know why she went for the throat. I think I'd aim for a spot with more meat, the chest or the belly. The neck is such a small target; you might miss completely, and I doubt it would be very satisfying, even if you did hit it. If you were that angry, wouldn't you want to tear his guts out or something? And there was one more queer thing: that same day, a patient was murdered at the hospital where the doctor worked. A woman who was just about to have heart surgery. The attacker used a pair of scissors, stabbed her in the chest. I wonder whether there's a connection between the two? Something more complicated than a simple crime of passion? Oh, yes! I nearly forgot. And a reporter from one of the talk shows came around asking questions, too. How could they resist?—it's a perfect story. But it was a shock, having a camera shoved in my face. I recognized the reporter, one of those fast-talking women with too much makeup. No one in the neighborhood had seen anything, so she was having trouble digging up information. But I told her everything I knew about the woman upstairs. That she was beautiful, wore designer clothes . . . Oh! Also she followed the recycling rules of the building. I only knew her from saying hello in the elevator. But the reporter seemed really grateful; she said my information was very useful. Of course, they'll hide my identity when they put it on TV. No one wants to have their face splashed around in connection with something as awful as this. She said the interview would be broadcast tomorrow. I'll have to record it. Who knows, maybe what I told them will turn out to be the key to solving the case. Do you think so?"

I was out of breath from talking so much. At some point he had let go of my hand.

We fell quiet after that, but it was an uncomfortable silence, different from the peaceful moment we had been sharing just a few minutes ago. The wineglasses shone on the table. Steam was rising from the pot on the stove. And the noises upstairs had stopped.

"Do you find it amusing that someone died?" he asked.

"Oh, I forgot to make the coffee," I said, pretending I hadn't heard him, and then ran to the kitchen. I clattered the cups against the door of the cupboard as I took them out, hoping the noise would break the silence—and deflect his question. But it was no use.

"Do you find it amusing that someone died?" he repeated in the exact same tone, now standing in the doorway of the kitchen, arms crossed.

"What do you mean?" I said. "There's nothing amusing

about it. It's just that I . . ." But before I could finish, he grabbed his coat and walked out, slamming the door behind him.

I'm not sure how long I sat there, alone. The water boiled, but I realized I no longer needed it. I put the coffee cups back in the cupboard. Then I went out.

I had no intention of running after him. It was as though he had already gone somewhere far away, and I could run and run but I would never catch him.

What had I done to deserve such treatment? I may have let myself get a little carried away, but I didn't think there was anything funny about the murders. I was truly sorry about what had happened. I'd been very serious when talking to the detective and the reporter. If I got excited, it was just because I was so happy to see him.

In the end, I guess my explanations were no use—there was no one to hear them anyway.

It was a weekday afternoon, the plaza in front of the city hall was almost empty. The ice-cream cart and balloon vendor came only on Sunday. A man was taking a nap on a bench. Some young people were reading on the steps in front of the clock tower. The bakery where I bought the cakes this morning was quiet now. A flock of pigeons flew into the air and then settled around a bench.

Four o'clock sounded, the door in the tower opened, and the wooden figures—soldier, rooster, and skeleton—marched out for their little parade. A few tourists gathered around to take pictures.

Since my boyfriend and I had usually met at the plaza, I had seen the show so often I was sick of it. Especially since he was usually late.

The angels appeared with golden wings fluttering. The left wing on one of them was loose and looked like it was about to fall off, while the jaw of the skeleton seemed to be stuck. Paint was chipping from the rooster's comb. I knew every last ugly detail.

The angel at the back of the line turned on its spool, the skeleton rang the final bell, and the door closed. The tourists wandered off. I skirted the tower and took the road behind the city hall. Most of the souvenir shops were closed.

I had a friend once who was dumped by her boyfriend because he didn't like a coat she had bought. It was a very nice cashmere coat, but for some reason it disgusted him to see her wearing it. At least that's what he told her. She cut it up, doused it in lighter fluid, and burned it, but her boyfriend never came back.

Another girl I know lost her boyfriend for using eyedrops in bed. They were just normal drops, but he said he couldn't stand seeing her put them in. Strange that a little thing like a coat or an eyedrop can ruin everything.

I walked for a long time, turning down narrow and deserted streets, hoping to avoid people—because every time I saw another person, I thought it might be my boyfriend. I passed the library, a dry cleaner, a beauty parlor that had gone out of business. A little playground with just a swing and a sandbox. A hedge of Red Robin. A puppy playing in the grass. At some point I lost sight of the clock tower.

When I finally got tired of walking, I stopped in front of an old stone house. A huge oak tree grew in the front yard. There were lace curtains in the windows, and bright red flowers in the planters. An elaborate design had been carved into the paneling on the front door. There was no sign of anyone in the house, only the sound of oak leaves rustling in the breeze.

The rusted sign on the gatepost was hard to read, but I managed to make out the characters for "Museum of Torture." Just the spot for me right now.

Bright colors streamed in through a stained-glass window high above the lobby. There was a curved staircase at the back of the room. An umbrella stand with a mirror, two high-backed chairs, a piano that looked like it hadn't been played in years. A hat rack and a few other carefully arranged pieces of furniture. The rug on the floor was soft and deep. An empty vase had been set on a side table, and a porcelain doll with curly hair sat on one of the chairs. A lace runner with a pattern of swans covered the shoe cupboard. Everything was very elegant.

But the air was stale, as though the room were holding its breath, and the only thing that moved was the light from the windows when the oak leaves fluttered outside.

I looked around for a reception desk, but there was nothing like that—no pamphlets or arrows showing where the tour started, no ticket machine or anything else you might expect to see in a museum. The doors on either side of the lobby were closed.

I screwed up my courage and called out, "Excuse me!" To be honest, I wasn't sure I wanted to see the Museum of Torture, but for some reason I couldn't stop myself. After all, torture might have been better than going home to my silent apartment.

"Excuse me!" I called again, but my voice seemed to die away. I thought for a moment, and then chose the door on the left. I always go left when I have to choose. He was left-handed.

"Welcome," said an old man in a bow tie. He held out his arm to show the way, as though he had been expecting me. But I was startled and froze for a moment. "Please come in," he said, running his hand through his white hair. His cologne smelled like a fern. The handkerchief peeking out of his breast pocket matched his tie; his cufflinks were set with pearls.

"I tried calling from the lobby, but no one answered. I apologize for barging in like this."

"Not at all," he said. "But tell me, have you come to see the collection? Or are you here to contribute a piece?"

"A piece?" I said.

"An instrument of torture," the man answered, smiling just a bit. I shook my head. "I see," he said. "Very well then, I would be happy to give you the tour."

We were standing in the living room. The furniture included a pair of couches; a claw-foot cabinet; a long, narrow table like something from a church; a rocking chair; and a record cabinet. There was a real wood-burning fireplace at the end of the room.

It was a fancy room for a rich man, the kind of place I'd like to live in myself. But there was one strange thing about it: every bare space was covered with some device for torture.

They were crammed in the cabinet and lined up on the table, stacked in the bay window, on the mantel, under the chairs, behind the curtains. Even hanging on the walls.

"Are all these yours?" I asked.

"No," he answered, as though the idea seemed ridiculous. "I simply look after the collection. I give tours for our visitors, take care of the items on display, and appraise new acquisitions. We have to guard against fakes and forgeries."

"Is there a difference between the genuine article and a fake when it comes to things like this?"

"Why, of course there is. We consider an item genuine only if it was actually used to torture someone. If it was simply intended as a decoration, it's a fake." Then he turned and pointed at the wall. "Well then, shall we begin here?"

A set of four iron rings, each dangling from a chain, had been mounted a few feet off the floor. It looked like some prop for a magician or a circus act. The metal was rusted and there were brown stains on the wallpaper behind it.

"The rings would have been placed around the victim's hands and feet, and then horses would pull the chains in different directions. It's a fairly conventional device, used in France at the beginning of the eighteenth century. In later years, the horses were replaced with winches, so the pain could be inflicted in more carefully calibrated increments, which is the whole point when it comes to torture."

The old man had pronounced the words "carefully calibrated" with special care.

"Next we have this leather strap and these pliers. The victim's wrist was attached to a table with the strap, and the pliers were used to extract the fingernails. Note the unusually delicate tips of the pliers."

It might have been a trick of the light, but the strap looked wet. The pliers seemed almost harmless.

"This house was owned by twin sisters, daughters of a coal baron. They were maiden ladies who lived well into their eighties, and they traveled the world assembling this collection."

"But what did they want with all this?" I asked. "Rich people usually collect paintings or jewels or things like that."

"The desires of the human heart know no reason or rules. I suppose I might ask you instead what you hope to discover by coming to see us today?" He coughed and put his hand to his throat, as though about to straighten his bow tie. I caught another whiff of his cologne.

"You said that people bring things to you, to add to the collection?"

"That's right. From time to time, patrons come to us with items they've discovered. I examine them, and if they seem suitable, I purchase them and put them on display."

"But how can you tell whether they're genuine or not?"

"First, I test the age of the materials: iron, wood, brass,

leather, fabric, tin. An object may look old, but only the proper scientific testing can reveal its true age. Then I have to determine whether the instrument has actually been used or not—but that's generally far easier than testing the age. You simply have to check for the presence of blood."

I looked back at the rings and the fingernail pliers and wondered whether the spots on the wall and the moisture on the leather strap had something to do with blood.

"If you're ready, we can continue," the old man said.

No one joined us for the tour. I was alone with the old man for what must have been hours. Every room had been turned into an exhibit space—the kitchen, the library, the living room, the bathroom, the study—and yet it was almost as if they were still in use. There were spotless quilts on the beds, the smell of vanilla in the kitchen, and a book open on the desk in the study. But torture was everywhere.

The old man was good at his job. He could rattle off the history of each object without missing a beat, and it was obvious that these things meant a lot to him.

As I followed him from exhibit to exhibit, the only sound in the house was our footsteps. I caught glimpses of the garden when we passed a window. The sun was beginning to set.

He was tall and his shoulders were broad. His voice was firm and he moved like a much younger man. I thought for a moment that I might have been wrong about his age—but when I looked closer, I could see the spots on his face and the wrinkles on his neck.

What was I doing here? And what was my boyfriend doing now? The shrimp had been in the marinade too long, and the strawberry shortcake would be getting stale. It was too late.

But somehow the sight of all these instruments of torture, all of this pain, seemed to fit right in with thoughts of my boyfriend.

"This was brought to us by a bag maker." The old man pointed at another object.

"It's like a corset," I said, peering into a cabinet he had opened in the living room.

"It is indeed. It's cowhide stretched over a whalebone frame. The device is fitted over the torso and gradually tightened until the ribs crack and the internal organs are crushed. It was designed specifically for use on women."

"May I touch it?"

"Yes, of course."

"It doesn't look particularly old," I said.

"You're quite right, it isn't. It's actually something that the bag maker designed himself. But my testing revealed traces of human flesh on the inside of the tube, so I found it worthy of being exhibited."

I pulled my hand away and wiped my fingers on my skirt, trying to avoid letting him see what I'd done.

"Don't worry," he said. "The quantities of tissue were infinitesimal."

"I was actually afraid I might be destroying precious evidence," I told him.

I wondered which would be more painful: to have your throat slit, to have your heart gouged out, or to have your chest crushed? I bet it's the corset, since you probably could last a while even after your organs burst. I wondered, too, about the woman who lived upstairs from my apartment. Had she been arrested yet? I imagined that nice detective using the corset to extract a confession. He could make her talk. He certainly was interested in what I had to say, unlike my boyfriend.

There were bright tiles in the bathroom, a new bar of soap in the dish, and neatly folded towels. A shaving set and jars of makeup were lined up above the sink.

"This item is somewhat rare. It comes from southern Yemen." The old man seemed to be gaining strength as he went on.

"It's just a funnel," I said.

"Yes, but a special one. The victim is immobilized on his back, and the funnel is used to drip cold water on his face, one drop at a time."

"And that's torture."

"It most certainly is—one of the more brutal, in fact." He picked up the funnel and held it carefully in both hands. It was made of a dull silver metal almost the same color as his hair. "For a torture to be effective, the pain has to be spread out; it has to come at regular intervals, with no end in sight. The water falls, drop after drop after drop, like the second hand of a watch, carving up time. The shock of each individual drop is insignificant, but the sensation is impossible to ignore. At first, one might manage to think about other things, but after five hours, after ten hours, it becomes unendurable. The repeated stimulation excites the nerves to a point where they literally explode, and every sensation in the body is absorbed into that one spot on the forehead—indeed, you come to feel that you are nothing but a forehead, into which a fine needle is being forced millimeter by millimeter. You can't sleep or even speak, hypnotized by a suffering that is greater than any mere pain. In general, the victim goes mad before a day has passed."

He returned the funnel to its place in the exhibit.

What did my boyfriend's forehead look like? It had usually been hidden under his long hair, but I had certainly seen it when he was getting out of the shower, or when he pushed back his bangs with that unconscious swipe of his hand, or when his head bobbed violently over me in bed.

I was sure that beautiful forehead would look lovely under an endless drip of water. Icy drops, cold enough to numb the skin, falling right on his forehead, then running down his face and disappearing into his hair. Like he's crying. With another tear ready at the mouth of the funnel. His eyes are closed, his lips tensed. His forehead is so cute I have the urge to kiss it. But I can't touch him, I can't give him relief from the drops.

"Now this one is absolutely unique," the old man said. "We are especially proud of it." He held up what appeared to be just another ordinary pair of tweezers. There were stains where the fingers would have held them.

"The pain inflicted resembles that of the funnel we've just seen, but of a coarser variety. These were used to extract the hair from the victim's head, one strand at a time."

"I'm not sure I understand," I said.

"I suppose it does seem a bit strange," he said, nodding

and touching his tie again. "The hairs are extracted one at a time, a procedure requiring infinite patience and perseverance. Until the scalp is completely exposed.

"It's horrible to lose one's hair. When the Nazis brought prisoners to a concentration camp, the first thing they did was to shave their heads in order to strip them of their humanity. In reality, it does no physical harm, but we seem convinced that our very existence is somehow bound up in our hair."

"You're right," I said. "I'm a beautician. I should know."

"Then you'll understand the nature of the torture. It is conducted in a room lined with mirrors. Thus, no matter how hard the victim tries to avert his eyes, he is forced to watch himself becoming bald. The process is time-consuming, but it's important that the hairs be removed one at a time. If you rip out several at once, the effect is lost. The suffering comes from the slow but steady sense of loss—along with the tiny pain the victim experiences each time a hair is plucked. It's nothing at first, but as it's repeated a thousand times, ten thousand times, a hundred thousand times, it becomes the most exquisite agony imaginable."

The rich colors of the sunset were cast down on us through the skylight. The breeze had died and the leaves of the oak tree were still. The evening shadows collected under the old man's eyes, making his smile seem a bit spooky.

The next time my boyfriend comes over, I'll give him a haircut on the balcony. I'll cover him with a plastic cape and put a towel around his neck. And then I'll tie his arms and legs to the chair. Maybe this old man will lend me some straps. They've got plenty to spare. The ones with the fingernail tweezers would do.

And then I'll pluck out his hair. It probably doesn't matter where you start—behind the ears, or maybe on the top of the head. They'll flutter down like insects with long wings. I'll enjoy that tiny bit of resistance each time I pluck a hair, the feeling of the skin ripping, of fat popping to the surface.

Before long his scalp will appear, soft and white and delicate. Like the skin of the hamster I found in the trash can. The hair will pile up until the breeze sends it swirling around his legs. If a strand sticks to his face, he won't be able to brush it away. He won't be able to do anything but groan. He won't be able to stop me doing just what I choose.

"I hope you enjoyed your visit."

"I certainly did. Thank you for the tour," I said, bowing. "Would you mind if I asked one last question?" He nodded. "Do you ever get the urge to try out some of the things you've got here?"

He put his hand to his temple and stood looking at the light in the lobby.

"Of course I do," he said at last. His smile had disappeared. "In fact, I don't exhibit an object unless I have the desire to use it." He ran his hand through his hair.

"Would you mind if I came back sometime?" I asked.

"By all means," he said, smiling once more. "Whenever you feel the need, please come to see us. We'll be expecting you."

THE MAN WHO SOLD BRACES

Everything my uncle touched seemed to fall apart in the end. The plastic model airplanes he helped me build when I was a boy, the braces he sold through the mail that were supposed to make you taller, and even the fur coat he left me when he died.

He was the sort of man who changed professions like other men change their socks. He worked for a while at a hat factory, and then became a photographer's assistant. Next were the braces, followed by a stint teaching table manners. He was a butler for a while, and finally a curator at a museum—though I may have mixed up the order somewhere. In the midst of all this, he was married three times, with several affairs in between. The women came and went, but in his later years he lived alone with no one to look after him. In other words, my uncle never seemed to think twice about abandoning a job or a woman to start over from square one.

If he had one admirable quality (and I'm not sure you could call it that), it was his ability to look dispassionately at the thing that lay broken in his hands, the thing he was about to lose or discard. He never seemed glum or sulky over his losses. He just watched calmly as his treasure, whatever it might have been, vanished from sight—and in many cases there was even the hint of a smile on his face as he watched it go.

I got a call from the police telling me my uncle had died and I should come to claim the body. He had no acquaintances among his neighbors and only a very few relatives, and the police had apparently gone to some trouble to locate me. I had just got back to my dormitory and was preparing for my French class when the phone rang.

"How did he die?" I asked.

"Strangulation," the person on the other end of the line said.

"You mean he was murdered?"

"No, I'm afraid he was crushed under the garbage that had accumulated in his apartment, the poor soul." I took some comfort in the sympathetic tone of this unseen caller.

My uncle and I were not in fact blood relatives. We thought of him as my mother's older brother, but he came into the family at the time of my grandmother's second marriage and was actually the eldest son of her new husband and another woman. There was also a large age difference between my uncle and my mother, and they had apparently never lived under the same roof. This relationship was explained to me any number of times when I was a child, but I had never understood it very well.

In any event, my uncle was a frequent visitor at our house. He would appear without warning, stay a few days, and then disappear again to parts unknown.

Even as a child, I sensed that he was not a particularly welcome guest. My mother would be nervous the whole time he was there, and my father was noticeably irritable. But my uncle seemed oblivious to all this: he was quite cheerful and ate and drank with great appetite.

I, too, was largely unaffected by my parents' attitude toward him and looked forward to my uncle's visits with impatience—primarily because he never failed to bring me some rare and unusual present.

"Now where could it be hiding?" he would say, picking me up in his arms and rubbing his cheek against mine. "Do you think you can find it?" If I squirmed away from his prickly beard, he would rub even harder. Eventually I would manage to get free and search him for my present—a procedure that was also my opportunity to tickle him.

One time I found a bar of imported chocolate in his hat; on another occasion it was a miniature model car up the sleeve of his jacket, or a jackknife tucked in his sock. When I was very young, I believed he produced all these things by magic.

The sheath for the knife was inlaid with semiprecious

stones. It was solid and heavy in my hand, and just looking at it sent shivers down my spine. But when my mother found it, she took it away from me.

"What could he have been thinking, giving a dangerous thing like that to a child? He has no common sense at all." That was what she always said about him.

Even if he wasn't always welcome, the menu at dinner was a bit fancier when my uncle was visiting. I would crawl into his lap as he sat cross-legged at the table and pretend not to hear when my mother scolded me for it. His legs were quite boney, but for some reason I felt comfortable seated there.

On such evenings, my uncle generally did most of the talking. My father did not drink and was, by nature, somewhat taciturn. My uncle would talk about new business prospects or some strange adventure from his travels, or he would gossip about the family. As he spoke, his voice and gestures were almost theatrical, and he would laugh merrily at his own stories. From time to time he would feed me some tidbit that had been served with his sake. My father said little and asked no questions, content to look on with a bemused smile, while my mother simply shuffled back and forth to the kitchen.

Eventually my father would make some excuse about an early start in the morning and leave us. I was told to put on my pajamas, and my mother would begin to clear away the dishes—but my uncle would linger on at the table.

And if I got up in the night to go to the bathroom, he would still be sitting there—with his whiskey, slumped over the table and mumbling incomprehensibly. But from time to time he would sit up and laugh to himself, the same laugh we'd heard all through dinner.

During the day, he would loaf about the house. Whenever my mother asked him to help with some chore that required physical strength, he would respond enthusiastically, although she would rarely ask him to do more than carrying a box of my father's books to the second floor or opening the sticky lid of a jar. Clearly, she did not consider him very useful.

When he got bored, he would wander over to my room.

"Well then, shall we build that model?" he once proposed.

The model in question was one my father had bought me for my birthday. He and I were planning to build it the following Sunday. I was suddenly filled with anxiety; not so much over breaking the promise to my father, but because I just knew my uncle would ruin the model. He seemed completely unaware of my feelings as he tore open the box and spilled out the parts.

"Let me help," I urged.

"No, this is pretty tricky. A bit much for a kid. You'd better let me do it." I was not permitted to touch the propellers or the wings or even the tube of glue.

The instructions were printed in a tiny typeface, and he was constantly adjusting his glasses or moving the lamp as he worked. He spread out the pieces on the desk and fitted them together, then pulled them apart again. He would put them together another way—and then start over with a different set of pieces, muttering the whole time about how confusing it was.

"Is everything all right?" I asked, overcome with nerves.

"Be patient," he said, nodding. "It's going to be fantastic." A bead of sweat dangled from the end of his nose.

Unable to stand it anymore, I went outside to play. When dinnertime came, he was still working on the model—which bore only the vaguest resemblance to an airplane.

"It's all right if you don't finish it," I said, trying to be as diplomatic as I could. Unfortunately, he was not about to give up. It was sometime the next morning before he was done.

"There," he said, coming to find me with the plane in his hands. "What do you think?"

"It's great," I said. It looked nothing like the photograph on the box, but I was reluctant to disappoint him. Traces of glue clung to his fingers.

The plane was oddly out of kilter, as though none of the pieces were in quite the right place. The cockpit had gaps, the wheels were askew, and, worst of all, the wings had been attached at crooked angles.

My uncle left after lunch that day. Later, as I was setting the model on top of my bookshelf, the right wing fell off. I let out a little cry and the propeller dropped to the floor, followed by one of the wheels, and finally the left wing, which came to rest at my feet.

———

One day my uncle appeared with an odd-looking object. It resembled a dog's collar that had been attached to the end of a long, narrow metal plate. At the other end was a wide belt.

"This is a brace to make you grow," he said. My parents looked skeptical but said nothing. "Let me show you how it works."

I was chosen to be the guinea pig.

"Does it hurt?" I asked, somewhat alarmed, but my uncle just shook his head and started loosening the buckles.

"Not a bit," he said. "You'd like to be taller, wouldn't you? Short guys never get the girls—which is why men all over the world are going to be clamoring for these."

The belt that looked like a collar turned out to be exactly that. My uncle buckled it tightly around my throat. The metal plate pressed against my spine, held in place by the belt around my waist.

"How does that feel?" He spread his arms and studied me with obvious satisfaction, but there was a concerned look on my mother's face. And, indeed, I was finding it hard to breathe; my neck was being forced up, and I couldn't turn my head to the side or bend at the waist. I was completely immobilized, with only my eyeballs free to move.

"Just thirty minutes a day for six months and you'll be two inches taller. It stabilizes the neck and pelvis and stretches the muscles, which provides stimulation for the bones and encourages secretion of the growth hormone."

"Thirty minutes?" I said, nearly in tears.

"And you'll be taller. What more could you ask?"

"But it hurts," I said. "I can't breathe."

"You can't?" he said, fiddling with the buckle. "I guess I've got it too tight. This is just a prototype; I'm still working out the details. But I've decided to go into the mail-order business with these, I'm completely convinced they'll sell. I've signed a contract with a factory to produce them, and I'm going to advertise in all the newspapers and men's magazines. I'm even applying to have them licensed as a medical therapy."

He pulled some papers out of his pocket and waved them in front of us.

"Is that so?" my father said, sounding even more skeptical than usual. My mother tapped her finger against the metal plate.

"Take it off, please! I can't stand it anymore." I was crying in earnest now.

Not long thereafter, true to his word, my uncle began selling the braces through the mail. I have no idea whether he ever fixed the collar, but I started seeing his advertisements in magazines: a shirtless man with well-oiled muscles in my uncle's brace, striking a confident pose. When I'd worn it, the brace had been terribly uncomfortable, but it seemed to fit the model like a second skin, as though he had been born wearing it.

The prototype sat in the corner of my closet for some time after that, like the molted skin of some misshapen reptile, but I never put it on again. Eventually, the metal plate started to rust. When my mother went to throw it out, the screws in the plate came loose, the belt fell off, and the whole thing went to pieces.

My uncle apparently sold almost none of them at all. I'm not sure whether it was because they broke so easily or because they failed to live up to their advertising, but very soon my uncle was arrested for fraud. It seems the license he had obtained was a fake.

It was some four years later, when I was in middle school, that we next heard from him. Looking back, I suppose this was probably his most prosperous period. The clothes he wore—and the quality of his presents—improved considerably. He smoked cigars, wore French cologne, and he seemed always to arrive at our house by a hired car.

He said he had found work as the butler in a great house, though my mother said she couldn't imagine he was anything more than a handyman. The house in question belonged to two elderly ladies, twins who had inherited a considerable sum from their father—a coal magnate of some sort. Since they spent most of their time traveling, my uncle's duties consisted primarily of standing guard over the house.

I recall that one of my aunts spread the rumor that the two old ladies shared my uncle's sexual services between them. At the time, I couldn't conceive of what this might mean, but she seemed disgusted when she said it, so I knew it was nothing to be proud of.

"They're absolutely identical," my uncle said. "From the build and voice to their taste in clothes and makeup, even their wrinkles. Exactly the same."

"Do you ever get them mixed up?" I asked.

"No, there's really nothing to mix up. A or B, B or A—it makes no difference. They're just one person."

"But what does a butler do?"

"My job is a bit different from your average butler." His tone was boastful as ever. "Mostly, I look after the Bengal tiger."

"Tiger?" I blurted out.

"That's what I said. He lives in the garden. They got him when they were traveling in India, while he was still young."

"But he got big?"

"He got huge! So huge you can't get your arms around him, and his legs are like iron poles. The claws could tear you apart, and the ground shakes when he walks across the yard."

"Aren't you scared?"

"Sure I am! That's why I have to be on my guard all the time. He could charge at any moment, but that danger is what makes him so beautiful. His fur shines and the stripes on his back ripple, and there's this deep rumble in his throat. He's absolutely perfect, but it's the kind of perfection you can't touch, even when it's right there in front of you."

He closed his eyes, as though trying to remember every detail of the tiger.

"To tell the truth, the biggest problem with the tiger is the odor—it's overpowering. It gets into your pores, right down the roots of your hair. That's why I always wear my cologne. It was a present from one of the ladies. Not sure which one. Anyway, it cost plenty." At this point, he moved closer until his chest was almost touching my face. "Nice, isn't it?" he said. He had apparently acquired expensive tastes from living among the wealthy, though the experience had made him no richer himself.

"But the old ladies are really more interested in all different kinds of torture," he went on without opening his eyes. "They go all over the world, buying anything that could be used to inflict pain, and my job is to take care of all the things they bring home."

"That's a pretty strange job," I said.

"At first I thought it was torture enough being left alone with the tiger, but I have to admit that some of the devices they bring back are pretty interesting: a hatchet for breaking ankles, a stretcher to rip open your mouth, a knife for flaying human skin."

He described these "devices" one after the other, and I found it difficult to picture what they looked like. Some of them, though, reminded me of that brace of his.

The image of my uncle that remains clearest in memory for me is of his back as he is leaving our house. No one ever knew where he was going, and no one asked. He left with little more than a "See you later."

When he returned, he was carrying nothing. He never had a suitcase, and I wondered what he did for clean underwear and the like. Perhaps he kept these things tucked away somewhere in his pockets—like the gifts he brought me.

"I've had a wonderful time," he would tell us when he was ready to go again, and he apparently meant it. And then he might tell me how important it was to study hard. "Even if something seems pointless at the time, you mustn't take it lightly. You'll see how useful it is later on. Nothing you study will ever turn out to be useless. That's the way the world is."

He would pick me up and rub his cheek against mine. Sometimes I would struggle to escape and muss his carefully combed hair in the process, but he never seemed to mind. Then he would bow and thank my parents, smoothing his hair with his hand.

"When will you be back?" I would ask. It still amazes me that I could have been so blunt as a child—but I truly wanted to know.

"I wonder . . ." He was incapable of making promises of any sort.

His last visit was after the old ladies had died and the house was turned into a museum of torture, for which he was to serve as curator. I was by then too old for our little games.

That time, too, a hired car came to take him to the station—spotless, black and impressive. He tripped on the front stairs, and when I went to help him he thanked me in a raspy voice. I caught a whiff of his favorite cologne.

It shocked me to realize that he suddenly seemed old—so frail that the slightest push would have sent him tumbling. The body I had felt when I'd gone searching for my hidden presents had been sturdier; and though I had always thought of him as tall, he was now much shorter than me.

I realized I had no idea how old he was—I suppose I'd thought that something as mundane as age could never apply to him.

"Give my regards to the tiger," I said, leaning in the car window. He nodded, but it was unclear whether he had heard me. "My regards to the tiger," I said again. He had no other family in the world, as far as I knew.

He waved with his usual theatrical flair, like a king bidding farewell to courtiers. When the car finally pulled away from the curb, I could see him through the rear window, thin and frail and growing smaller in the distance.

"Well then," said my father, turning to go back into the house. My mother followed him, nodding and muttering. I stayed behind to watch until the car was out of sight. He never turned around.

The funeral was over quickly. Only a few people had attended, and no one cried. They just took their turns lighting incense in front of the family altar, looking a bit lost. Not lost in grief; they seemed to be lost in thought, wondering perhaps what they were doing in such a place.

"They said he wasn't murdered but he died of asphyxiation," I heard someone whisper. "It seems odd."

"He was terribly weak," said another voice. "A wardrobe fell and trapped him underneath."

"I bet someone pushed it over. He had plenty of enemies."

"They said he was nothing but skin and bones, he would have starved to death anyway."

His troubles had started when one of his neighbors told the police that he was bringing underage girls into the Museum of Torture and doing indecent things to them. In fact he had been involved with an eighteen-year-old woman, a beautician, who had moved into the museum. But she never filed a complaint against him and the whole thing had eventually blown over.

"I'll bet he was torturing her," my father said.

"Why do you say that?" I asked, a bit shocked.

"The place was full of that stuff. What else could they do with it?"

But almost immediately after that affair was over, the police arrested him for embezzling from the old ladies' estate. He had apparently gone through quite a bit of their money in the few years since their deaths, and so, for a second time in his life, my uncle found himself in jail.

Worse still, they closed the museum while he was away and he lost his home.

He had asked me repeatedly to come visit him while he worked there, but I never managed to make the trip. I'm not sure why; I didn't dislike museums in principle and I wasn't trying to distance myself from him. I suppose I was preoccupied with my studies and extracurricular activities, and in the end I missed my chance.

He sent me a card every Christmas with a photograph of himself posing in front of the museum displays. Bow tie, starched shirt, his chest puffed out. He was usually pointing at one of his treasures, smiling happily; he seemed to be assuring the viewer that the device was a genuine instrument of torture.

I saw him for the last time in February, after he had been let out on parole. The clouds were low and the wind had been blowing hard all day. I had wandered for a long time, hands in my pockets, head bent in the wind, searching for his apartment. What I found at last was practically a ruin: a long, squat building with two lines of unadorned windows. No flower boxes, not even laundry hung out to dry. The walls were stained, the gutters pulled loose in places, the banisters crooked. It was perfectly silent except for the mewing of a cat hiding in the weeds near the door.

I checked the mailboxes to be sure I hadn't made a mistake. My uncle's name was written in magic marker on the box for number 201—though the characters were shaky and smeared by the rain. Peering in the box, I saw nothing but darkness, not a postcard or even an advertising flyer.

I opened the door to the apartment. "Uncle!" I called. "Uncle! It's me!" From somewhere inside, I heard the sound of labored breathing. I took off my shoes and slid open the inner door, but then I froze, unable to find a place to set my foot. The entire apartment was filled with a mound of garbage—though "garbage" wasn't exactly the right word for it. These were objects that had once been useful but were no longer so. A mountain of random things, with no discernible connection between them.

"Oh, you've come." His voice sounded weak, muffled as

it was by the mound of clutter. "Well, don't stand there all day. Come and let me look at you."

"I'd like to, but I'm not sure how," I said.

"Not to worry," he said. "Just come past the refrigerator, by the radio, slip behind the chest, and you're there." Following his instructions, I made my way cautiously into the apartment.

Worn-out socks, barbecue utensils, a set of encyclopedias, pieces of a clarinet, cans of cat food, pots without handles, dried-up bars of soap, a microscope, a marionette, a stuffed weasel . . . The sheer variety of items made me dizzy. Tightly packed in a giant mass, they filled the entire room, covering the windows and piled nearly to the ceiling. But somehow I managed to find him inside of it all.

"It's true, you're really here," he said. "But come closer. My eyes are bad and I want to get a look at you." He was stretched out in a tiny space near the middle of the room, all but buried in his things. His trembling hand reached toward me. I took it and held it to my cheek.

"I remember that face," he said. "And those soft hands. You haven't changed a bit." He, however, was nearly unrecognizable. He had grown terribly thin, his collarbone and shoulders jutting out sharply. I held tight to his hand.

"Thanks for the Christmas cards," I said.

"I don't send them to anyone else anymore."

I hesitated a moment, but then I decided to push back the things near his head and I knelt beside him.

"How are you getting along?" I said. I wanted to talk to him about the disaster in his apartment, but I didn't know how to broach the topic.

"I can't complain. Though the cold makes my neuralgia act up."

He was wrapped in a thin blanket, more a towel really, and so filthy that its original color was impossible to guess. There was no sign of a heater anywhere—but I had the feeling that this mass of objects gave off a warmth of its own.

"You haven't come to see us," I said.

"I know, there's always something . . ."

"Are you eating?" I asked. "You have to keep up your strength."

"All of a sudden you're grown and worrying about me, instead of the other way around. Seems like yesterday you were just a little boy."

"I'm at the university now."

"What are you studying?"

"French literature," I told him.

"Wonderful! Absolutely wonderful." He closed his swollen eyes and squeezed my hand, apparently on the verge of tears.

"Oh, I almost forgot. I brought you a present. Can you guess where I've hidden it?" Not wanting to see him cry, I forced myself to sound jolly. He let out a sound that was something between a cough and a laugh, and I produced a box of chocolates from the inner pocket of my jacket. "Weren't these always your favorites?"

"They were indeed," he said. "Thank you. But I never thought I'd see the day when you would bring me presents."

I balanced the box on a toaster, resting on a tricycle,

and almost immediately it blended in, becoming part of the pile.

As I studied the mass more closely, I began to feel that it was not the product of random accumulation but that it actually had a coherent form all its own; and while the individual items were dirty and deteriorating, taken together they were like a strange piece of art.

Something else became apparent: many of these scraps of wood and chains and leather were, in fact, the remains of exhibits from his museum. A twisted belt with buckles nearly torn off might have been used to bind the wrists; a whip with a broken handle; a rusted weight that could have crushed bone. But they were ruined, no longer suitable for causing pain; the devices themselves almost seemed to be the victims. They looked exhausted, ready to die.

I looked down at my feet and realized I was staring at the brace. The feeling of suffocation came back to me in an instant—the sweat under the collar, the plate against my back. Then I saw that he was lying next to a knot of old braces that looked impossible to untangle.

"I remember those," I said, and my uncle seemed to know what I meant without even turning his head.

"You do?" he said. "That was a great invention, even if it didn't sell. I still get New Year's cards from clients who are taller thanks to those braces. They think of me as their benefactor, and when I see them, I feel as though my life hasn't been a complete waste."

He closed his eyes, pulled his blanket up to his chin, and curled into a ball. When he coughed, a shudder ran down his back.

The wind blew outside, rattling the windows. A tiny creature—a mouse or a cockroach perhaps—scurried along the edge of my vision before disappearing into the instruments of torture. There was a quiet rustling and then silence again.

"Take one with you, if you like. I have plenty. Who knows, it could still help."

"Thanks," I said.

The kitchen was at the back of the apartment, but there was no sign that it was in use. The sink was filled with dozens of empty cologne bottles.

"Whatever happened to the tiger?" I asked.

"He died in the garden," he said. "It was a beautiful death."

We were quiet then for a moment. The only sound was the wind at the window. His arms reached out from under the blanket. I took his hands in mine, and it seemed to me that we were praying for the tiger.

"It's started to snow," he said sometime later.

"How can you tell?"

"The wind has died."

"Do you have a heavier blanket? You need to keep warm."

"I'm fine like this," he said. "You're the one who'll catch cold. You should wear this home," he said, plunging his hand into the mound next to him and pulling out a fur coat.

"It's wonderful," I said. "You should use it for a blanket. I don't need it."

"Don't say that. I want you to have it. It's the only thing I have to leave you."

"Well then," I said. "Thank you."

He closed his eyes again and a look of satisfaction spread over his face. A few minutes later his breath fell into the regular rhythm of sleep.

Where had it all come from? Outside, the world lay under a blanket of white, just as my uncle had said. The air was still, and large snowflakes drifted out of the night sky. The street was empty, and the cat that had been lurking near the entrance had disappeared. I walked gingerly over the unmarked snow. When I turned to look back, the window was dark.

Thanks to the coat, I didn't feel the cold at all. I felt as though I were being embraced by big, strong arms, and with each step I caught a whiff of my uncle's cologne. The fur was so soft, I found myself rubbing it against my cheek.

I wasn't sure how to get back, and the snow had covered and obscured all landmarks, so I could do nothing but walk straight ahead. The flakes that fell on the fur melted almost immediately. I turned one last time, but the building had vanished, and a trail of my footprints in the snow stretched back into the darkness.

Then I realized that the left sleeve had fallen off the coat. As I picked it up, I noticed a loose string hanging from it—and a large black stain on the lining. Before I knew what was happening, the right sleeve dropped off, too, and the cold crept in. I walked along, clutching the sleeves, but then the seams at the sides began to come apart as well. The collar came loose and the pockets fell off.

The fur shimmered in the white snow as I knelt to gather up the scattered bits of the tiger.

THE LAST HOUR OF THE BENGAL TIGER

I left the bypass and followed the road south along the river, then hesitated just as I was about to cross the bridge. If I turned and headed downtown, I could be at her apartment in just a few minutes.

It was a stifling afternoon. The breeze had died and the trees along the avenues seemed to wilt in the heat. The air shimmered above the burning asphalt; the sunlight reflected from the oncoming cars was blinding. Even on full, the air-conditioning did little against the heat coming through the window. The steering wheel burned my hands.

I had been playing a game with myself from the moment I left the house. If the next stoplight was red, I would make a U-turn and go home. If the silver sports car passed me, I would keep going. If the terrier puppy I'd seen yesterday in the pet shop window had been sold, I'd turn back. If there were more than three buses parked at the terminal around the next corner, I would go on to her apartment.

I'm not sure why I found myself hoping that the sports car would turn off, that the cage would be empty. I seemed to believe it still possible to turn back, despite my apparently firm decision to confront her.

Just before I reached the bridge, the traffic suddenly slowed to a crawl. It was probably an accident, since they had closed one lane. I turned on the radio, but the reception was so bad I turned it off again. I rode the brake as we inched forward.

What was I going to do when I saw her? It was a question I had asked myself a thousand times. Slap her? Scream insults? Demand she give my husband back? How ridiculous. It would be better to lose him than look so utterly foolish.

Good afternoon. I would probably just wish her "good afternoon" like an idiot, as though she were a teacher at my daughter's kindergarten.

My husband had left for the United States three days earlier to attend a medical conference. I would never have found the spine to do this if I thought I might actually catch him at her place, so I waited until he was gone before setting out. I wasn't really looking for a confrontation with the two of them, and I don't think I would have been especially upset even if I had found them naked in each other's arms. That was, after all, what they had been doing in secret all along. That much was obvious. I simply didn't want to make things more complicated than they already were, so it was better to see her when he wasn't there, when the two of us could sit down and discuss matters calmly and equitably. Or so I had been telling myself.

What was the name of his conference? I'd forgotten. My husband's specialty is respiratory medicine, specifically the treatment of a syndrome called pulmonary infiltrates with eosinophilia, though I don't really know what that means. He hasn't bothered to explain it to me, and I'm not particularly interested in finding out. But I suspect she knows. She's a highly regarded secretary at the university hospital.

I know it's ridiculous to be jealous about the name of a conference, but not about seeing them naked together, but that's just the way it is. Jealousy seems to make me suffer in the most unexpected ways.

The traffic crept along. A family was having a cookout under the bridge, and the smell of roasting meat wafted down the road, making the heat seem even more oppressive. Some seagulls were preening themselves, perched on posts in the sandbar. The river was dotted with windsurfers and small fishing boats. At the sound of an impatient honk the gulls fluttered up into the air. As I squinted into the sunlight I could see the ocean shining in the distance.

A truck had overturned on the bridge. It was probably going too fast and had hit the median. At any rate, the cab on the driver's side was crushed, and a tire had come loose and jumped the guardrail. An ambulance and a wrecker and several police cars were pulled up at the scene with emergency lights flashing.

I was pretty sure the driver was dead. His bones and organs would have been crushed by the steering wheel. But somehow this seemed less shocking to me than the fact that the surface of the road was covered with tomatoes. Not that I realized what they were right away. At first I thought I must have driven into a field where an unfamiliar red flower was blooming. Or that the driver's blood was covering the whole road.

But it was tomatoes—flawless, ripe ones—shining in the sunlight. A workman with a shovel was trying to gather them up, but he was making no visible progress. A number of people stood near the accident looking dazed, and some men were trying to cut open the cab of the truck with an electric saw.

Some tomatoes rolled in front of my car and must have been crushed under the tires, but I could barely feel them. They offered no resistance, as though they had wanted to be smashed all along, smeared across the road.

The other cars swerved to avoid the tomatoes, but I decided to try to hit as many as possible. If I got more than ten, I would go on, I would follow the road where it led. In the rearview mirror, I could see a strip of crimson stretching out behind the car. Did hitting tomatoes feel the same as hitting a person? I began to count: one, two, three, four, five . . .

I've seen her only once, from a distance. My husband had forgotten some research notes he needed for work, and when I went to take them to him, I stopped by the secretarial pool and peeked in. I knew right away which one was his girlfriend, even though I had never seen any of them before. I knew because she fit so perfectly in the various scenes I had imagined on the nights he failed to come home—a room in some apartment, a table at his favorite restaurant, the deserted lot behind the hospital.

Still, I have no memory of the face I saw that day. I can't recall how she wore her hair or makeup. The only thing I remember is that she was busy with some sort of complicated task.

She was standing at her desk, sorting documents. Thumbing through them impatiently, she would write on some, tear others to pieces, and attach labels to still others. Her face was half hidden by her limp, sweaty hair. When the phone on her desk rang, she called rudely for someone else to get it. Finally, it seemed she had finished putting all the papers in order, but then something must have happened because she made a disgusted noise audible even from where I stood and started the process again from the beginning.

But no matter how many times she started over, it didn't seem to work out. Something always went wrong. She was constantly erasing things she had just written, folding and refolding, stamping something here and there—as though trying anything that came into her head. But the longer she worked—and it seemed as though she might go on forever—the more chaotic the papers became. Nor, through all this, did anyone come to help her.

At last I gave up and left the hospital. I had wanted to see her discharging her duties in an elegant manner, efficiently typing one of my husband's papers. But how could I feel jealous of someone so pathetic?

I pulled into the parking lot behind the city hall, intending to walk the short distance to her apartment. I could have found a spot on the street closer to her building, but a parking ticket on a day like this would have been too depressing.

Apartment 508 . . . five-oh-eight. I muttered the number to myself as I climbed out of the car into the sweltering heat. Almost instantly, I was dripping with sweat. The powder I had applied with such care began to melt under the blazing sun.

As I walked, I recalled, one by one, all the times I had ever been rejected. This process had become something of a ritual with me since my husband's affair had started. I would unearth memories, beginning in childhood, of places and occasions when someone had hurt me. In that way, I believed, I would see that my pain was due not only to my husband but to the cruelty of countless others besides. I found it somehow comforting to think that his coldness was in no way special or unique.

At first I could recall only two or three instances. But as the connections between them became more apparent, the number grew and the details became more vivid. One by one, incidents I had completely forgotten came back to me as if from nowhere.

In kindergarten, when we paired up to dance, I was always the only one without a partner. I would end up dancing with the teacher, which was terribly humiliating. With an odd number of students in the class, why would the teacher have insisted on dancing in pairs in the first place?

Then there was the time before the class trip when my name was left off the list of room assignments for the inn where we were to stay. I thought I must have missed it the first time, so I checked again. No mistake: my name wasn't there. Of course, I told myself, it was unintentional, a simple oversight, but my rationalizing did no good. In the end, I didn't go on the trip. Not because of the list, but because I woke up that morning with tonsillitis.

At fifteen, I took an overdose of sleeping pills. I must have had a good reason for wanting to kill myself, but I've forgotten what it was. Perhaps I was just fed up with everything. At any rate, I slept for eighteen hours straight, and when I woke up I was completely refreshed. My body felt so empty and purified that I wondered whether I had, in fact, died. But no one in my family even seemed to have noticed I had attempted suicide.

Then yesterday, at the hairdresser's, when I asked the stylist to trim in back a bit more, she gave me this nasty look and clacked her scissors as if to say I had no business telling her how to do her job. And she was a young girl, probably just a trainee.

When I looked up again, I realized I was lost. I had studied the map carefully, but it seemed now as though the city had warped in the heat. Each time I turned a corner, the scene that appeared was different from the one I remembered. The people passing by stared gloomily at the pavement; a stray cat crouched in the shadows of an alley.

Rows of roofs stretched into the distance, and beyond them I could see just a glimpse of the back of the tower. The clock struck two. Though the day was still, the sound seemed to swirl around somewhere high above me before reaching my ears.

When the echo died away, I suddenly noticed an odor in the air. It was sweet and persistent but not at all unpleasant. I took a deep breath and let myself be guided by the smell.

"Fern," I murmured.

I was standing in front of a large stone house. The heavy iron gate was half open. A massive oak cast a cool shadow. Without a moment's hesitation, I went in. I walked toward the house, looking up at the windows, then passed around to the back on the west side. The smell was coming from there.

I found a beautiful and meticulously tended garden. Shrubs trimmed with amazing precision lined little green paths. A few blooms still clung to the climbing roses, and clear water flowed from a fountain at the center. Next to the fountain, a tiger lay sprawled on the ground, and next to the tiger crouched an old man.

"What are you doing?" I asked.

"Come see," said the man, who was apparently not at all surprised to find me standing there.

"Is it dead?"

"No, not yet," he said, waving for me to come closer.

As I approached the fountain, I felt a pleasant breeze. Small birds chirped, and it seemed as though the heat that covered the town had suddenly abated.

The tiger was enormous, stretched out against the curve of the stone basin. Its legs were limp, its mouth half open. Its breathing was weak and labored.

"Is it sick?" I asked.

"Yes, it won't last long." The old man held the animal's paw as he knelt beside it, and he seemed so comfortable and confident that I felt no fear. He gestured again for me to approach. He was dressed very formally for a hot summer day, but he did not seem to be sweating at all. He wore an elegant jacket, a bow tie, and pearl cufflinks. His white hair was neatly combed.

I knelt beside him and found I couldn't resist the urge to rest my hand on the tiger's back. The smell I had thought was fern seemed to be coming from the animal.

I was struck by the warmth of his body. This was no stuffed beast or a figment of my imagination but a living creature. Its hot mass pulsed under my palm.

"It's magnificent," I whispered.

"Magnificent indeed," the man said as he continued to caress the beast. Its black and yellow fur shone in the light filtering down through the trees. The beautiful stripes, the enormous size—everything about the animal was perfect.

Even lying prostrate, it seemed to be coiled and ready to attack; the paws looked heavy. The jaw was powerful, and sharp fangs peeked out from its mouth. Every bit of the tiger seemed to have a purpose, to be ideally suited to the hunt.

"It is yours?" I asked.

"It is." The old man nodded. A shudder ran through the animal's belly and it groaned.

"Poor thing," I said. I tried to concentrate my energy in the hand stroking the tiger's back. The fur was very thick and soft and pleasant to the touch. The more I stroked it, the more the scent of ferns filled the air.

"There now," the man murmured. Then he turned toward me for the first time and smiled.

The tiger's ears drooped and its tongue rolled from its mouth. It began to drool. With its last remaining strength, it pushed closer to the old man.

"There now," the man repeated, wrapping his arms around the tiger's neck and rubbing his cheek against its face.

The roses swayed in the hot breeze. Tiny insects danced above the lawn. Spray from the fountain misted down on us.

"I'm afraid I'm disturbing you," I said, realizing that I was intruding on their last moments together.

"Why would you say that?" the old man said, a hint of reproach in his tone. "You must stay with us. We need you here." Then he looked back at the tiger, his eyes full of pity.

The tiger's breath grew fitful. Its throat rattled; its fangs clattered together. The tongue looked rough and dry. I continued to rub its back; it was all I could do.

The old man held his cheek against the animal's head. The tiger's eyes opened and sought his face. When it was satisfied that he was still nearby, the eyes shut again in relief.

Their bodies had become one. Cheek and jaw, torso and neck, paw and leg, bow tie and stripes—everything melted together into a single being. The tiger let out a roar, and as the echo died away so did the beating under my hand. The clicking of fangs stopped, and a final breath seeped from its lungs. Silence descended on us.

The old man continued to hold the animal in his arms. I rose as quietly as I could and left the garden.

I put the key in the ignition and looked down for a moment at my palms. I wanted to remember what they had just done. Then I turned the key. On the way back, the tomatoes were nowhere to be seen.

TOMATOES AND THE FULL MOON

I checked in at the front desk and picked up my key, but when I opened the door, I found a strange woman and her dog in my room. The woman was sitting up very straight on the sofa, her hands resting on her knees.

"I beg your pardon," I said and hastily checked the number on the door and my key again. There was no doubt about it: room 101. "I'm sorry, but I wonder if you haven't made a mistake," I said, as politely as I could.

The woman seemed completely unabashed and not even particularly surprised. She simply stroked the head of the dog—a black Labrador lying quietly at her feet.

"Where did you come from?" the woman said at last. Her voice was much like a young girl's, so ill matched to her age and appearance that I found myself momentarily at a loss for words.

"I just checked into this room," I managed at last.

"So did I."

"Then the hotel must have made a mistake. We should probably call the front desk. Would you mind showing me your key?"

"Key?" she said, tilting her head and staring at me as though I had used some obscure medical term.

"Your key," I repeated, beginning to get annoyed. I had not slept the night before due to a deadline, and I had been caught in traffic on my way to the hotel. I was exhausted and just wanted to take a shower and go to bed as soon as possible. "Yes, the key to this room," I added.

"Oh, of course. I was just looking for it. I'm sure I left it over there, but I can't seem to find it . . ." She pointed toward the dresser but made no move to get up. The dog yawned and wagged its tail.

The woman fell silent again and sat as still as a doll. In fact, everything about her was doll-like: her tiny figure, her porcelain skin, her bobbed hair. Her wrists and fingers and ankles were so delicate they seemed as though they would break if you touched them.

"How did you get in here?" I asked.

"From the patio," she said, pointing in the direction of the French doors.

The sky was clear outside, the sun blinding. The lawn, damp from the sprinklers, glimmered in the light. Children could be heard shouting from the pool across the way; and beyond the pool, the glasslike sea was visible in the distance. A small bird perched for a moment on the back of a patio chair and then flew away.

"The door was open and it seemed like too much trouble to go around through the lobby—so much easier to come in this way, don't you think?" She was smiling now.

"I suppose so," I said. "But I'm afraid you've made a mistake. This is my room." As I said this, I threw my bag on the bed for emphasis.

"Oh dear! I'm terribly sorry. I'll be going right away." She clasped a bundle wrapped in a silk scarf under her arm, took the dog's leash in her hand, and stood up. Now that she was finally on her feet, she seemed even smaller. The dog shook itself and fell in at her side.

I held the door as they made their way outside and quickly vanished in the dazzling light. They left behind nothing but a few black hairs on the carpet next to the couch.

I rose early the next morning to drive to the tip of the cape and take pictures of the sunrise. Then I went to the fish market to gather material for my article. As I was entering the hotel parking lot, I spotted the woman again.

She was standing by the kitchen entrance, her bundle under her arm. In the other hand, she held a basket brimming with something red. The dog was still at her side.

I pulled into a space and stopped. After folding up my map and returning it to the glove compartment, I got out and made my way across the lot, pretending I hadn't seen her. I didn't really know the woman—barely enough to nod politely should I encounter her again. She was the one who had mixed up the rooms, so there was no need for me to go out of my way to be polite. Or so I told myself.

But I soon realized I couldn't take my eyes off her, that I was in fact spying on her between the parked cars. Somehow she seemed out of place here, not like the usual guest at a resort hotel; something about her set my reporter's instincts on edge. Or perhaps the sad look in the dog's eyes simply made me want to find out if there was something I could do to help.

"No, please," the woman was saying to the man at the door, who appeared to be a cook. "Take them." She was trying to hand him the basket. "We grow them organically on our farm, but we have so many we don't know what to do with them. We'd be delighted if you could use them."

I realized at last that they were tomatoes. The cook raised his hands awkwardly and looked embarrassed, as though unsure whether to take them or not. The woman continued to hold the basket out to him. Finally, the cook accepted some tomatoes, though he seemed to take them just to be rid of her.

"Please, as many as you want. It's nothing, really. Don't think a thing of it." She smiled with apparent satisfaction. Then, dog in tow, she turned and made her way through the cars in the parking lot and disappeared toward the sea—without ever so much as glancing at me.

The dining room was crowded, filled with children's voices and clattering dishes. The hotel seemed to be booked solid with young families on vacation. The sea was visible through the spotless windows.

Chandeliers in the shape of seashells hung from the

high ceiling. The blue of the tablecloths matched the color of the carpets, which were splotched here and there with sand brought in on the guests' sandals.

I was shown to a small table hidden behind a pillar. I ordered coffee, two pieces of toast, an omelet, bacon, and a green salad. The toast was warm; and I had no complaints about the bacon or the coffee either. But the eggs were oddly runny. I had ordered a plain omelet, but for some reason the one that arrived was stuffed with diced tomatoes. The salad, too, was covered with tomatoes . . . no doubt the ones that the woman had forced on the cook.

Just as this thought was occurring to me, I heard a voice.

"Is this seat taken?" She had appeared out of nowhere, smiling broadly. Her bundle was clutched to her chest; the dog's leash was wrapped around her wrist.

Startled, I choked on the egg and managed only to cough in reply. A moment later she was seated across from me, her bundle on her lap.

"You should drink some water," she said, sliding a glass toward me. I did as she'd suggested. "I'm sorry about yesterday," she continued. The dog made itself comfortable under the table.

"Not at all," I said, going back to my omelet.

"I'm afraid I upset you," she said.

"It's a common enough mistake."

"It's a comfort to hear you say so," she said. After that, she was silent for a moment. I started on my salad, and she watched me eat.

As she fiddled with the sugar bowl, I noticed again

that her fingers were unusually delicate. Her bony shoulders were visible under her blouse and her collarbones protruded above the neckline.

"Are you on vacation?" she said at last.

"No, I'm here for work."

"Really? What sort of work?"

"I'm writing an article about this hotel for a woman's magazine."

"Oh, how lovely!"

I was getting sick of the mountain of tomatoes in my salad. She eventually finished with the sugar bowl and began folding and unfolding a paper napkin.

"They haven't come to take your order," I said.

"Don't worry about me," she said, adding another crease to the napkin. Her eyes never left my face.

"I'll call the waiter," I said, starting to signal him over, but she rose out of her chair and touched my arm. Her fingers were icy.

"I said you needn't bother. I'm not hungry." She fell back in her chair and I went on eating my salad.

"Do you like the tomatoes?"

I nodded and she let out a little laugh.

"They're my little *contribution*," she said. The omelet lay half finished on my plate, surrounded by yolky tomatoes.

"I know," I said, forcing down the rest of the egg. I wanted to escape as quickly as possible.

"I picked them up yesterday," she said. "On a bridge." My knife scraped disagreeably on the plate. I pretended not to hear. "A truck driver apparently fell asleep at the wheel and his truck turned over. You should have seen it:

the bridge was covered with tomatoes. I couldn't resist picking up a few. I'm afraid the driver died, though: the cab was crushed, and I suppose he must have been, too."

I set my knife and fork on the plate, wiped my mouth, and then balled up my napkin and dropped it on the table. But before I could move, she rose from her chair.

"I'm sorry to have bothered you," she said, and glided away through the crowded dining room.

For the rest of the morning, I was shown around the hotel by an assistant manager and allowed to take pictures of the three grades of rooms they had available: standard, deluxe, and suite. Bathrooms, decks, closets, amenities, slippers, minifridges. I took pictures of everything, from every angle I could think of, while the manager babbled on about the beauty and comfort and luxury of the hotel.

Then in the afternoon I went to check out the beach. A sky-blue sign in the shape of a dolphin stood at the entrance to what was named, appropriately enough, Dolphin Beach. Lines of umbrellas, snack stands, and public showers, and the cape running out beyond to the east side of the bay. Tour boats were tied up at a dock.

"What time does the dolphin-watching boat leave?" I asked a young woman who was selling shaved ice topped with syrup.

"Excuse me?" she said. Her tone suggested my question was unexpected or unwelcome or both.

"Dolphin-watching boats?" I repeated, a little louder this time. "It's right here in the brochure."

"They're dead," she said as she drizzled bright yellow liquid over a cup of ice. "All three of them."

I sighed and shouldered the heavy pack I used to carry my camera equipment. The "D" and the "i" in the name of the boat were illegible; the chain to the dock was covered with dried seaweed.

After a couple of drinks at the bar, I took a walk behind the hotel. A full moon had turned the sea to liquid gold. The tennis courts and the archery range were deserted. A curtain was drawn at the reception window and the lights had been turned off. A dirty wristband was left lying on the ground. I cut across a putting green and climbed a hill planted with grapevines, my way lit by the moon. There was no breeze, but the midday heat was beginning to die down.

At the top of the hill, there was a small bench, a broken spyglass, and a greenhouse. I sat down on the bench. The sea was calm, and no one was down on the sand or in the water.

Then I heard footsteps on the grass, followed by a rustling sound and the soft clink of a chain. I knew who it was without turning around.

"Good evening," she said.

"Good evening," I answered. Though there was almost no room on the bench, she sat down next to me. Her tiny body somehow fit right next to mine. As always, the dog was at her feet, the bundle on her lap.

"Has your work been going well?" she asked.

"Well enough," I said.

"What sorts of things do you write about?" she said, cocking her head and turning to look at me. She was wearing a plain skirt and blouse with no jewelry—except for the dog's leash, which was wrapped around her wrist like a bracelet. Her cheeks were pale and translucent, and there were fine wrinkles at the corners of her eyes. She clutched the bundle in her carefully manicured hands.

"'The moment you enter, you feel you've stepped into paradise. Each Mediterranean-themed room has an ocean view. The staff is warm and the service impeccable. The beach is just seconds away, and the gentle surf is perfect for the kids. As an added attraction, you can go swimming with the dolphins just offshore . . .' Something like that," I said. "It's pretty much the same for all these places—and I suppose I won't mention that the dolphins are dead."

I tapped my toe on the ground. The Labrador sneezed. His black coat melted into the darkness.

"Yes, I heard about that," she said. "It's an epidemic—a parasite attacked their lungs." The moonlight shone on her face as she looked out at the sea. The pounding of the waves could be heard even at this distance.

"Why did you come up here?" I said, but as soon as the question was out of my mouth, I realized how rude it must have sounded.

"Am I disturbing you?" she asked.

"No," I said, shaking my head. "That's not what I meant."

"You look just like a man who once saved my life," she said, tucking her hair back to reveal pale ears. "It happened nearly thirty years ago. I was lost in a snowstorm. It had come down very heavily. Then the wind died and the world was very still. Much like tonight." She looked up at the night, as though waiting for snow to fall out of it, but only the moon and stars were in the sky.

"If I had been alone, I think I would have died quite peacefully, without much of a struggle—or many regrets. But I wasn't alone then. I had a child with me, a dear boy of ten. So I couldn't die; I had to escape somehow."

"Yes, I see what you mean," I said.

"Do you have children?" she asked.

"I do. My son is ten as well."

"My, what a coincidence."

"But my wife and I separated when he was three, and she hasn't allowed me to see him since then."

"Oh . . ." she said. We fell silent for a moment and listened to the sound of the sea.

"We were on our way home from the zoo," she continued. "It was terribly cold and we had been the only visitors. I remember exactly the sort of coat the boy was wearing, the pattern on his scarf. He asked me why the giraffe's neck was so long. He said it was 'absurd.' How did a ten-year-old child know a word like 'absurd'?"

"He must have been very intelligent," I said.

"He was, and I was so proud of him. At any rate, the snow kept falling and we were hungry. It was getting hard to walk, and he started feeling dizzy. He never complained, he just kept walking, but I could tell from how he gripped my hand that he was afraid."

She stared at her palm, perhaps trying to remember the feeling of the boy's hand.

"The road was deserted, but then the headlights of a car came out of the darkness with no warning at all. It pulled to a stop right in front of us, as though the driver had been out in the storm looking for us. 'Can I take you home?' he said. He was terribly polite—much like you."

"Did he really look like me?"

"Exactly. I realized it the moment we met. The way you wear your hair, your eyes, your chin . . . you're identical."

I sat perfectly still as she reached over and traced my profile with her fingertips. Her cool, slender hand lingered for a long time on my face.

That night I dreamed about parasites wriggling in the dolphins. With each breath, their long bodies quivered in unison—like the motion of the woman's finger. Blood oozed from the lungs.

The weather forecast said it would be the hottest day of the summer so far, but the pool was chilly and refreshing. Some birds were flitting about on the terrace, drawn by breadcrumbs from the tables. Umbrellas would be opening on the beach before long.

I was doing leisurely laps in the pool, practicing the crawl stroke. A blue dolphin had been painted on the bottom, giving the illusion that the water itself was bright blue. The morning sun was blinding as it reflected off the glass.

I lost count of my laps after about four hundred meters. The dolphin watched me with big, round eyes, its tail flipping at a jaunty angle. A fine stream of bubbles rose from a chlorine tablet dissolving on the bottom.

I was just reaching the wall of the pool and preparing for my turn when I heard the sound of applause. I stopped at the edge.

"You're very good. I thought you might go forever." She was sitting on a deck chair under an umbrella. "Can you do other strokes?"

She wore the same skirt and blouse as the day before. The dog lay at her feet. A waiter with a tray of drinks passed between us. I did three laps of breaststroke and two of backstroke, and the applause grew louder.

"Marvelous!" she said. "Like an Olympic swimmer."

No one was paying attention to us—not the children laughing and clinging to tubes in the pool, nor the woman in a bikini applying sunscreen, nor the man on the lounge chair reading the newspaper. Only the woman and her dog seemed impressed with my performance.

"And the butterfly?" she said. "Or is that outside your repertoire?"

"Not at all," I said, and I did a lap of butterfly as well. The spray flew and the children took refuge in the far corner of the pool. The buzz of conversations around the pool came and went as I plunged in and out of the water. The chlorine tablet continued to shrink.

"Bravo!" shouted the woman, rising from her chair and clapping. The dog wagged its tail.

The hotel library was on the first floor of the annex building, facing west to a garden. The walls were lined with bookshelves and there were a few furnishings—a desk, a couch, and some rocking chairs. The books were all quite old: the collected works of various novelists, anthologies of poetry, thick tomes of botanical prints, picture books, a volume on American country cooking, a study of black magic in the thirteenth century, a dictionary of business English . . . Some of the bindings were beginning to fray and the spines were faded.

"Could you turn a little to the left?" I said.

"Does my hair look all right? I combed it before I came." She sounded a bit anxious but also excited to be having her picture taken.

"You look fine," I said, clicking the shutter. "Like a professional model."

The library was empty. Not a single guest had wandered in to find a book. A breeze gently tugged at the curtains in the window. The sun streamed in through a skylight, illuminating the woman and the dog at her feet.

"Try to relax," I told her. "Just pretend I'm not even here."

As I took the picture, its caption appeared in my head: "While away an afternoon in the quiet of the hotel library." I wondered how many books they had here—something to check later with the assistant manager.

"Would you mind putting down your package for a

moment?" I asked. "The shot might look better without it." She had insisted on keeping the bundle on her lap.

"No, I'm afraid I can't," she said, shaking her head.

"I'd be happy to hold it for you," I said, and reached out for the package. But she turned her back and clutched it still tighter. The dog snapped to attention and barked for the first time since I'd met them.

"I'm sorry," I said.

"It doesn't matter," she said, but the bark seemed to hang in the room for a long time.

"We're nearly finished," I said. "Just a few more. Are you getting tired?"

"Not at all," she said, resuming her pose. When I looked in the viewfinder again, she seemed to have become even tinier.

"I wonder why there's no one here?"

"I suppose it's too quiet for most people."

"But it's such a lovely library . . ."

"Shall I order something to drink from the lounge?" I suggested.

"Why don't we just sit a bit longer."

Outside, sunlight filtered down through the trees in the garden. The dog had dropped off to sleep.

"It was warm in the car despite the snow," she said, continuing her story as though she had paused only for a moment. "The seats were soft; music was playing on the radio. It was as if we had suddenly entered another world."

"It must have been a very nice car," I said.

"It was indeed, extremely comfortable. And as we rode, my son finally seemed to relax. He let go of my hand and began playing with the button lock on the door, wiping the steam from the window. In those days not everyone had a family car, so it must have seemed quite strange to him."

"But what was he like—this man who looked like me?"

"I don't really know," she said, staring down at her lap as though the fact caused her considerable pain. "I asked his name, hoping to thank him later, but he didn't tell me. I never learned where he lived or what he did or why he was passing by. The only thing I know for sure is that you and he are absolutely identical. Face, body—even your hands are the same as the ones I saw holding the steering wheel that night." I looked at my hands resting on the film case.

When the wind changed direction, I could hear the faint sound of laughter from the pool, but the books around us formed a wall of silence.

"What is your son doing now?" I asked.

"I haven't seen him since he was twelve," she said, tugging at the knot on her bundle. The silk was soiled and fraying in places from being carried about so much. "He wasn't really my son," she added. "He was my husband's child from a previous marriage. I've never had children of my own."

The dog half-opened its eyes and scratched its neck. Then it settled down again and went back to sleep.

"He would be just about your age now," the woman said.

"Then I seem to have all the parts in your story," I said. "Both your savior and your son."

"I suppose you could say that." Her smile was warm but a bit sad.

My body felt heavy from the morning's swim, and I thought I might drop off to sleep in the heat—like her dog—so I asked a question that had been bothering me for some time.

"What do you have in your bundle? It must be something very important."

"A manuscript," she said, gathering it up in her arms again.

"Well, don't worry," I told her. "I'm not going to touch it."

"You can never be too careful," she said.

"What sort of manuscript is it?"

"A novel. I'm a writer, and I couldn't bear to have it stolen. That's why I take it everywhere I go. You're a writer," she added. "You can understand how I feel."

"Of course, though in my case losing a manuscript wouldn't make much difference—no one cares what I write . . . So, did you come here to work on the book?"

"You could say that," she said. A cicada started to cry in the garden and then fell silent. The sun had slowly made its way across the skylight, leaving the dog in shadow. "When I'm away from home, they sneak in and try to steal what I've been writing. I went out to the supermarket, and when I got back the lamp had been moved and the papers on my desk were askew. The next day I took the dog for a walk and my eraser was on the floor and some pages were missing. I could tell someone had been there.

It was horrible. But it was no everyday burglar—he was after my manuscript." She spoke more quickly, her fingers working frantically at the knot on her bundle. "And then that hunchback woman with the glasses published a novel exactly like the one I'd been writing. The same plot, same characters, even the same title. Isn't that the most horrible thing you've ever heard?"

I nodded but said nothing.

"She pretended she'd written it herself and even had the nerve to give interviews. I read that she told them the book was the 'result of destroying the world [she] had built in all her previous works'—or some such nonsense."

She snorted and the tip of her tongue appeared between her teeth. It was shockingly red, like the tomatoes I'd eaten the day before.

"So that's why I carry everything around with me now. You never know when they'll try again. I've got eight hundred pages here; two hundred more and I'll be done."

She rubbed her cheek against the bundle.

"Do they have any of your books here?" I asked.

"They do," she said, standing up and going to one of the shelves. "This is mine—one that managed to escape the burglar," she said, handing it to me.

Afternoon at the Bakery. The book was slender, and as tattered as her bundle.

I worked on my article in my room until 7:30, phoned my editor, and then went down to dinner: bouillabaisse, salad, and a beer. The evening was still, but there were ripples on the surface of the pool. People were eating out on the terrace.

I had chosen the seat facing away from the view of the ocean, expecting her to appear at some point. I had even moved the extra chairs so the dog would have room.

There were no tomatoes in the salad tonight. I ordered another beer and ate the last few mouthfuls of bouillabaisse. But there was still no sign of her.

Later, in my room, I read "Afternoon at the Bakery." It was about a woman who goes to buy a birthday cake for her dead son. That was the whole story. I should have gone back to my article, but I read her novel through twice, finishing for the second time at 3:00 a.m. The prose was unremarkable, as were the plot and characters, but there was an icy current running under her words, and I found myself wanting to plunge into it again and again.

Inside the back cover was a short biography of the author—her date of birth, titles of her major works, and the fact that she had disappeared in 1997—and a picture of a woman I had never seen before. She wore glasses and had a hump on her back.

As I was getting ready for bed, I stopped to take a picture of my son out of my wallet. He was turning three when it was taken, just about to blow out the candles on his cake. He was holding a monster doll someone had given him. The corners of the picture were dog-eared, but I would never have a newer one.

"He'll be eleven this year," I said aloud. But there was no answer. The boy in the photograph was completely absorbed in his cake. I knew his age, but what good did that do me?

"Why don't you start with the backstroke?"

She sat under a cloudless sky, waving from the deck chair. I was not particularly good at the backstroke, but I managed a hundred meters. "Marvelous!" she called. The dog watched, his head resting between his paws. "Now the breaststroke. Four hundred meters."

"Four hundred?"

"I like watching you do the turns," she said. Sunlight glinted off the bottom of the pool. Legs crisscrossed in front of me; a child's inflatable ring drifted in the next lane. Fifty, seventy-five, one hundred . . . I kept track of the total at each turn.

"Four hundred!" I caught my breath for a moment, resting against the side of the pool.

"Wonderful!" she shouted, clapping on and on, the sound filtering down through the water. I took some pleasure in seeing how happy she was. "And for the finale, my favorite. The butterfly, if you please."

When I was finished in the pool, I had to go to the aquarium to get the last of the material for my article. I even considered asking her to go with me. The aquarium was said to own a dugong—a creature much like a manatee—if it hadn't died like the dolphins.

But when I completed the last lap of butterfly and

pulled myself up on the side of the pool, she was no longer there. The deck chair was empty; the dog, too, had vanished.

The dugong was alive and well and, when I arrived, was eating some lettuce. Later, when I returned from the aquarium, I took a moment to organize the film I had shot and to pack my suitcase. I had to check out before noon, and the article was due to my editor the next day.

"She was an older lady, small, always carried a bundle about this big." I held up my hands to show him, and the man behind the desk thought for a moment. "And she had a dog with her. A black Lab."

"Oh, I know who you mean," he said, nodding at last. "She checked out this morning."

"Are you sure?"

"Yes, quite sure."

But why would she have left without saying good-bye? Without praising my butterfly one last time?

I carried my bags out to the parking lot before going to have a final look at the pool. It was as crowded as ever, umbrellas jostling one another, waiters hurrying about with trays of drinks.

But the chair where she had sat that morning was empty, and on it was her bundle, looking forlorn and almost frightened. I picked it up and untied the knot. Inside was a ream of blank paper.

POISON PLANTS

The first time I met the young man was at a charity concert, just as a children's choir was beginning an encore of Brahms's "Little Dustman."

"Would you like another?" he asked, taking an empty champagne glass from my hand. His white suit—obviously rented—was too large for his slender frame.

"You have a lovely voice," I said, ignoring his question. "You should be in a choir yourself."

"Thank you," he said, smiling politely. "But I'm afraid my voice is not what it used to be." One rarely meets a young man at once so deferential and, at the same time, self-assured.

"A shame," I said. "Those little berets that they're wearing would suit you. Are you interested in music?"

"Yes, indeed. In fact, I'm hoping to go to the conservatory."

"If not to sing, then what for?"

"I'd like to be a composer."

"But why? When you have such a beautiful voice?"

The children had finished their performance and were filing off the stage. They were very well behaved—except for one little boy who couldn't stop fidgeting with his beret.

"Are you sure you wouldn't like another?" he said, holding up my empty glass. His hand was large and strong.

"Why not?" I said. I didn't really want more champagne, but I wanted him to come back to me.

The concert was organized by a local banker, a man who had bought a number of my paintings in the past. In the days that followed, I had him arrange a "scholarship" to help this boy with his studies. He had been wasting his time with odd jobs to make ends meet, so we came to an agreement. I would pay for the lessons he needed to prepare for the entrance exam to the conservatory, and he would come every other week on Saturday night to eat dinner with me and to report on his progress. I'm not sure he fully realized what this meant. Still, he did what I asked of him without complaint, and he even thanked me in that polite way of his.

I knew there was something arrogant about my little arrangement, but I also knew it wouldn't last for long. All too soon, the rest of his body would catch up with his hands—and just as soon I would be too old to lift a glass of champagne.

I remember the first visit well. It was a cold, windy night.

"What a wonderful house you have," he said, looking all around. He was dressed in corduroy pants and a heavy duffle coat.

"Sit down," I said. It was somehow unsettling to hear his pure voice—which I had heard only over the din of a party—here in the quiet of my home.

He sat at one end of the sofa and folded his hands in his lap. The little smile on his face seemed to ask what he should do next.

We moved to the dining room and ate shrimp cocktail and meat loaf. I had asked the maid to stay late to serve. He would eat a shrimp, take a bite of meat loaf, then take a sip of water, and in between he gave me a detailed account of his studies. The banker's instructions must have been very specific.

Thanks to my "scholarship," he had been able to add voice lessons and had found a new piano teacher who had connections at the conservatory. You might imagine that such things don't matter in the world of music, but in reality they make all the difference. He was also able to hire a tutor for music theory, and he described the man's peculiar insistence on sterilizing the desk and chair before the lesson could begin. He had started to attend concerts at least once a week, and had bought some reference works that had been too expensive before. Fascinating books, he said, terribly useful. He had brought receipts, he told me.

"I don't need receipts," I said.

"No?" He was out of breath from his long speech. He pressed his napkin to his mouth and then took the last bite of meat loaf.

I had no particular interest in his lessons or anything else he told me; I simply wanted to hear his voice, speaking now for me alone.

After dinner, we had tea in the living room. His report complete, he had little more to say. He stirred his tea cautiously and took a single cookie from the plate on the table. When our eyes met, he smiled faintly. I suspect he may have been worried about boring me—but bored as I have been by the silence in this big house for so many years, I found myself absorbed by the stillness, now that he was near me. I listened to the winter wind blowing outside.

"You have a piano," he said at last, gesturing to where it stood in the corner of the room. I almost thought I heard the piano let out a little cry, as though its strings had been plucked simply by his regard.

"My daughter used to play," I said. "I had it tuned for the first time in thirty years in honor of your visit."

"You have a daughter?"

"I did; she died when she was nineteen."

"I'm sorry . . ." he said, returning his cup to the saucer.

"You needn't be. Everyone I know has died. My past is full of ghosts."

The locks of hair at his temples threw shadows on his face. His nose was straight and finely shaped; his intelligent eyes seemed to drink in everything around him. And his lips looked so soft you wanted instinctively to touch them.

"Do you still paint?" he asked.

"No, I can't," I said, staring at his profile. "My hands don't work properly anymore." Despite the careful manicure and a ring—a present from an old lover—there was no denying that my hands were wrinkled and ugly. If I reached out for him, these hands would tremble with fear. And yet he took them in his and gently rubbed them, as though he believed his touch could restore their youth.

"Could you play something for me?" I asked. Releasing my hands, he went to the piano. The lid moaned as he opened it. "Something by Liszt," I said. "The 'Liebestraum,' if you don't mind." His fingers settled on the keyboard.

My young prince came without fail every other Saturday evening, precisely at five. As the weeks passed, we grew less formal with each other. He told me about his studies or not as the mood dictated. We talked about whatever captured our fancy. Often we would take a walk until it was time for dinner. We wandered through the park, or, when my strength allowed, we climbed the hill beyond to admire the sunset.

At such moments, he would seem quite grown up. He would take my hand—the one not holding the cane—and wrap his arm solicitously around my shoulder. "Lean on me," he would whisper in my ear, and those few words had the power to make me utterly content.

When it rained, we leafed through books of paintings, or I would show him albums of photographs and tell him about my past. Sometimes I told his fortune from the cards, and at those times he was once again the innocent little boy. He would hold his breath, hardly able to contain his excitement, as I revealed for him the significance of the numbers and pictures.

"Can you see what will happen in my love life?" he asked.

"Of course," I told him.

He wrote down his girlfriend's birthday on a piece of paper—just a few numbers, but they told everything about the girl's youth, and made me terribly sad.

After dinner we would sit quietly. Sometimes he would play records while I wrote letters, or perhaps we would watch a movie on the television.

But I was happiest when my prince read aloud to me.

"My eyes tire easily . . ." I would murmur, and I knew he would never refuse. He would sit to my left on the couch, since my right ear is a bit deaf, and begin from the spot where we had left off the last time. Almost any book would do. Historical fiction, science fiction . . . I would have been happy to hear him read the telephone book. I simply wanted to hear his voice, to savor its warmth, the feel of its vibration in my ears.

He read quietly, his tone almost flat, and sometimes he even stumbled over the words. But it made no difference. His breath, as he hesitated over a character, seemed to caress my face.

The hill was planted with fruit: a few grapevines and some peach and loquat trees. The rest was all kiwis. . . . The kiwis in particular grew so thick that on moonlit nights when the wind was blowing, the whole hillside would tremble as though covered with a swarm of dark-green bats . . .

He was reading a book from my husband's library. I've forgotten the title now. His lips pursed sweetly around the word "kiwi," as though they ached to meet mine.

I sensed the lingering warmth of the sun as I washed the flesh of the carrot. Scrubbing turned it bright red. I had no idea where to insert the knife, but I decided it would be best to begin by cutting off the five fingers. One by one, they rolled across the cutting board. That evening, my potato salad had bits of the pinkie and the index finger.

My prince never hurried, pronouncing each word with great care. His voice came from deep in his chest, yet it was soft and almost meek, and trembled ever so slightly at the end of a phrase. It filled the room like music, like liquid, and I felt as though I could reach out and scoop it up in my hands.

The post office was searched and found to contain a mountain of kiwis. But when the fruit was cleared out, it revealed only the mangy body of a cat. . . . As the sun fell behind the trees in the orchard, the shovel uncovered a decomposing body in the vegetable patch. . . .

His eyes never left the book, and he would continue to read until I stopped him. The slight rustling sound as he turned a page added to the charm of his performance. The downy hairs on his neck glowed gold under the light of the chandelier. His curls had grown out since we'd first met, half hiding his ears. The contour of his chest was visible under his sweater—a boy's chest that would soon be a man's.

I closed my eyes and let his voice wash over me, tracing his form in my mind in painstaking detail: his toes and calves, his hips, his arms, chin, lips, eyelids . . . And I felt his smooth tongue and long fingers run delicately over my body. The curls tickled my cheeks and I stifled a cry as his breath moved down along my side.

My hands were young again—no wrinkles, no trembling—and as he touched me I could feel the rest of me hurrying back to the past as well. I would be able to grip a brush again, to paint the picture I wanted. I would be able to wrap my fingers around his penis . . .

"What sort of man was your husband?" he asked, taking a photograph down from the mantel.

"I've forgotten," I said.

"You can't mean that."

"It's true. He's been dead more than forty years now and I've forgotten. I'm afraid it can't be helped. Forty years is a long time—you can't possibly imagine."

"He was handsome," he said.

"Don't be silly. You can't tell anything from an old picture."

"And you were very beautiful," he said—to me, forty years ago.

"He was wealthy. He hired me to do paintings of some

of the plants in his garden. There was a great difference in our ages. I was a poor art student, barely nineteen, a waif with paint on her fingers." He had slipped the bookmark between the pages and handed the book to me. I held it to my chest. "The plants I painted were all quite poisonous: wild sweet peas, locoweed, monkshood. When I finished the paintings, we got married."

He put on his duffle coat, tied his shoes, and bowed. "I've had a wonderful time." He said the same words each time he left me, and I believe he meant them. He turned again at the gate to wave. I kept my hands on my cane, but I nodded to signal he should go, and he would hurry off into the darkness to catch the last train.

Just once he tried to break his promise. He telephoned to ask if it would be all right if he didn't come on Saturday. I knew every nuance of his voice, and I could tell how nervous he was.

"Are you ill?" I asked.

"No, but I was wondering whether I could come Sunday instead."

"Is something wrong? Did something happen?"

"No," he said again.

"But tell me why you can't come. I'll worry if you don't."

"I'm sorry to ask, after all you've done for me."

"That's not the point," I told him. "I want to know why you can't come."

He was silent for a moment. "It's my girlfriend's birthday," he said at last. I remembered the date he had written down when I was telling his fortune, and the numbers and symbols on the cards.

"No," I said. I hadn't intended to say it, but the word slipped out.

"But her birthday is on Saturday."

"So is mine," I said. This was a lie, of course, and he knew it. "And who knows, I may not be alive to celebrate next year. I'll expect you as usual." Then I hung up.

My prince came on Saturday evening. "Happy birthday," he said. He had brought a small bouquet of flowers, the same ones, I supposed, he would have given to his girlfriend—yellow, fragile, they seemed to shudder as I put them in the vase and set them on the mantel. I had no idea what they were called, but they reminded me of one of the flowers I had painted for my husband long ago.

"Shall I continue reading?" He opened the book without being asked.

My cane struck a small stone and I fell, skinning both my hands. Blood oozed from the wounds, and the pain was terrible. One of my sandals came off and rolled into the grass. A spotted dog appeared from somewhere and began sniffing at it.

"Scat!" I called, brandishing my cane, and it backed away with a snarl. I managed to pull myself up on a tree, but the bark was rough against my skin.

I had been climbing the hill behind the park as we often had but decided to turn back before I reached the top.

Then I had lost my way and found myself in a part of the wood I did not know. One side of the path was a stand of fern in a bog; the other, dense undergrowth. The sun suddenly seemed low in the sky.

Not knowing which way to go, I chose a direction at random and set off. There were no maps of the area or arrows pointing the way. From time to time, a bird flew up from the bushes. The cuts on my hands were still painful, and my skirt was speckled with twigs and leaves and dead insects.

I had thought I was heading downhill, but the path started to rise again quite steeply. Still, I was reluctant to turn back.

"Lean on me." I thought I heard his voice, but I did not look around. He had not appeared for our next appointment. Instead I received a letter along with all the money I had given him for his studies:

". . . happy to inform you that I have obtained a scholarship from the Foundation for Musical Culture . . . and fully realizing your generous support could benefit someone with greater need . . . hereby return to you . . . with my most sincere thanks . . ." The tone was polite, but terribly cold.

I lost my cane as I was crawling up the hill. Bracing my foot on the roots of a tree, I took hold of a branch and barely managed to pull myself over the lip of a small ridge. The blood was clotting on my hands.

Then I found myself at the edge of an open field that sloped gently above me—a field covered with boxlike objects. I reached out to touch the nearest one: a refrigerator. Broken refrigerators—some upended, others half crushed, white ones, blue, yellow, big ones, tiny ones, some missing doors, some scrawled with graffiti—every refrigerator imaginable.

I wove my way through them, noting all the different ways in which they had been damaged, ruined beyond repair. The silence was oppressive.

My chest began to ache and cold sweat ran down my back. My foot caught on something and I stumbled again, managing to catch myself on a large, double-door stainless refrigerator, the kind from a restaurant kitchen. It was spattered here and there with bird droppings.

I opened the doors—and I found someone inside. Legs neatly folded, head buried between the knees, curled ingeniously to fit between the shelves and the egg box.

"Excuse me," I said, but my voice seemed to disappear into the dark.

It was my body. In this gloomy, cramped box, I had eaten poison plants and died, hidden away from prying eyes.

Crouching down at the door, I wept. For my dead self.

www.ingramcontent.com/pod-product-compliance
Lightning Source LLC
Chambersburg PA
CBHW021521310326
42179CB00013B/123